'Let's get down to brass tacks,' Thomas said.

'...e bo... new to the Port of Manchester, ...av... ...at in common, but it ends there. ...ce between us is that you know ...d I know plenty.'

...ch, Chloe thought grimly.

...s you will have to perform on ...ut every spare moment I have I ...ith you.'

a groan. That might be all very ...he job point of view, but she had ...t wouldn't do much for her self- ...or peace of mind!

Abigail Gordon began writing some years ago at the suggestion of her sister, who is herself an established writer. She has found it an absorbing and fulfilling way of expressing herself, and feels that in the medical romance there is an opportunity to present realistically strong dramatic situations with which readers can identify. Abigail lives in a Cheshire village near Stockport, and is widowed with three grown-up sons, and several grandchildren.

A PROMISE
TO PROTECT

BY
ABIGAIL GORDON

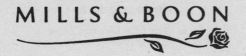

MILLS & BOON

With grateful thanks to the Chief Port Health Officer
and his staff of the Port of Manchester,
and also to some of the memorable men who sail
the Ship Canal and the River Weaver

*MILLS & BOON, the Rose Device and LOVE ON CALL
are trademarks of the publisher.
Harlequin Mills & Boon Limited,
Eton House, 18–24 Paradise Road, Richmond, Surrey TW9 1SR
This edition published by arrangement with
Harlequin Enterprises B.V.*

© Abigail Gordon 1995

ISBN 0 263 79396 6

*Set in 10 on 12 pt Linotron Times
03-9511-53873*

*Typeset in Great Britain by CentraCet, Cambridge
Made and printed in Great Britain*

CHAPTER ONE

CHLOE was smiling as she let herself into the apartment, a happy beam that was the outward sign of the excitement and satisfaction inside her. Once the door had closed behind her she flung her jacket across one of her mother's frail Regency chairs and hugged herself with delight, and then she was skipping across the thick rose pile of the carpet in a crazy jig, shapely legs whirling, arms outstretched, her short blonde bob lifting with the movements.

Although she hadn't yet been given it in black and white, the job was hers. The decision of the interviewing panel had been conveyed to her after the light luncheon that had been provided for the interviewers and applicants at the Port House beside the docks. She'd been up in the clouds ever since, a state that was propelling her into a mad dance among her mother's elegant furnishings.

She could still barely credit it. They hadn't chosen Natalie, who was just as qualified and capable as herself, and a lot more attractive, or the laid-back, over-confident Nick, who looked as if he'd stepped out of a mail-order catalogue, in spite of having already spent two years in a similar position to the one for which they were being interviewed. Nor had they chosen either of the two more solid-looking candidates whose faces had become a blur as she'd waited her turn to go before the panel.

They'd chosen *her*. . .Chloe Cavendish, with the small straight nose, and hazel eyes in a nondescript face. She was going to work on the waterway that had fascinated her for as long as she could remember, in the worthwhile responsible position of a port health officer.

Gone were the days when she'd stood behind the jewellery counter in an exclusive store, or tried to ignore aching feet as she'd waited to serve the choosy clientele of a fashionable boutique, or, as she'd done at one time, skivvied in one of Manchester's smart restaurants. The years of studying had paid off. She was going to get her teeth into something with job satisfaction. A situation where her training as an environmental health officer was going to provide her with the opportunity to help safeguard the health of the public and that of the seafarers who came and went through the Port of Manchester.

A key turned in the lock and Chloe became still. Her mother was back, and one thing was certain: there would be no joy on her behalf from *that* direction. As Lorraine Cavendish came through the door Chloe eyed her warily. She was small and fair like herself, but the resemblance ended there. Attractive in a pinched sort of way, her mother was heavily made up, and the clothes she had on in the mid-afternoon would have graced a royal garden party. For an insane moment Chloe tried to imagine her mother in a hard hat and waterproofs, skipping across the lock gates to inspect a tanker, but the vision refused to be conjured up.

'Well? How did you get on?' Lorraine asked, easing off a pair of soft leather gloves, and thrusting her feet into gold satin mules at the same time.

'I got the job, Mum,' Chloe told her carefully, and then, finding it impossible to batten down her enthusiasm any further, she whooped, 'I'm going to be a port health officer!'

Lorraine was eyeing her unsmilingly.

'So you've got your wish. You're going to be grubbing around that wretched canal for the rest of your working life.'

Idle and pleasure-loving herself, Lorraine had never seen any harm in her daughter earning her keep, but not like this, certainly not like this, Chloe thought grimly. Her mother wanted her to be employed in something more in keeping with her own image, glitzy and frivolous.

Her euphoria was disappearing fast. She'd known that Lorraine was against the idea of her working at the port from the start, but it hadn't weakened her resolve. In other matters she would fall into line for the sake of peace, because basically she was an uncomplicated sort of person, but on this issue she had stood firm, and now here was the backlash.

'*You've* never complained about that same waterway providing you with a life of luxury, have you?' she protested stiffly. 'It was the Manchester docks that made Dad's shipping firm prosperous. If it hadn't been for that, you wouldn't be swanning around like you do!'

'That is an entirely different matter,' her mother said icily, eyeing the daughter who frequently puzzled and displeased her. 'My point is that the ports are full of men. . .not young girls. There is an excellent opening for a receptionist at my health club. Why don't you go after that?'

Chloe swallowed hard. She didn't want today's success to be blighted by her mother's disapproval. They were as different as chalk and cheese. She'd inherited her own sturdy independence and dislike of fuss from her father.

'I'm not a young girl, Mum,' she said quietly. 'I'm twenty-eight years old, and I've done the rounds of the sort of jobs *you* would like me to have. Now, after four years of hard grafting, I've got my B.Sc. and am determined to do something useful with my life.'

Her mother gave an aggrieved sigh.

'All right. *You've* made *your* point. We've had this argument until it's threadbare. I suppose there is one person who *would* be pleased if he were here. Your father was drawn to that stretch of water, too, and we both know that you take after him.' Then, as if she couldn't be bothered to discuss it further, Lorraine draped herself across the nearest chair and said in a milder tone, 'Put the kettle on, Chloe. I'm gasping for a cup of tea.'

As she went to obey the request, Chloe breathed a sigh of relief. Thank goodness *that* hurdle seemed to have been crossed. Her mother now knew for certain what her daughter intended to do with her future, and, knowing Lorraine, Chloe was aware that although her disapproval wouldn't disappear it would only surface at such times as when she wasn't engrossed in herself, and those occasions were rare.

Chloe's throat tightened. If her dad had been here, *his* reaction to her news would have been so different. He would have understood her motivation and been proud of her, although, having said that, if he *had* been here none of this would have been happening.

Her function in the port would have been something quite different. She would have been already taken into the firm, involved in the trade that came with the waterway, working beside him in the red brick building on the wharf beside the Ship Canal. The building that had now been demolished to make way for prefabricated storage sheds. John Cavendish had died of a heart attack when Chloe was fourteen, and her mother had wasted no time in turning the business that he had founded into hard cash.

'I'll be doing the next best thing, Dad,' she whispered in the empty kitchen. 'Out there on the waterway doing a useful job, in the open, not chained to a till.'

On the interviewing panel that morning there'd been eight councillors from the riparian boroughs that bordered the canal, and the head of the port authorities. Her immediate superior, the chief port health officer, had also been present, but was not allowed to be involved in the final decision.

When she'd overheard over lunch that the choice had been narrowed down to Natalie and herself, Chloe had fully expected the other girl, with her obvious attractions, to be the lucky one but, unbeknown to her, one of the councillors had pointed out that they weren't looking for mannequins. They were looking for common sense and stability, the ability to cope in bad weather conditions, or in dangerous and unpleasant situations, with polite cheerful competence, and Chloe Cavendish appeared to have all those attributes.

There had been general agreement on her comments

and it had transpired that Chloe had been called back into the room to be informed that she would be commencing work as an officer with the Manchester Port Health Authority in two weeks' time.

After they had drunk the tea Chloe went to stand by the window. The spring afternoon was fading into early dusk and lights were coming on all over the city. To a lover of open spaces like herself, the penthouse apartment, in an exclusive complex that had once been a prestigious warehouse in the heart of Manchester, often seemed claustrophobic, but in the moments when a thousand twinkling lights appeared in the darkness, and the huge shadows of the other buildings loomed over the one where they lived, there was a brief haunting magic that lasted until the noisy nightlife of the city took over.

That was what Lorraine loved. The bustle and throb of the place, the wining and dining, the theatre, shopping for expensive clothes. Those were the things that filled *her* days.

If Chloe had ever thought to suggest they move to a cottage in the country Lorraine would have been horrified, and the prospect of leaving her mother, and branching out on her own, was always shelved because Lorraine couldn't bear the idea of living alone.

When Chloe became desperate for her own space, away from her mother's demands and suggestions, there was the beautiful Honda Fireblade waiting for her, and once she had straddled it and zoomed off tranquillity always returned.

Her mother had suggested she get a small car, but instead Chloe had come back with a motorcycle, known to bikers as the urban street tiger because of its gleaming beige finish decorated with fiery stripes.

Lorraine had been furious at the idea of her daughter becoming a motorcyclist, and when Chloe had joined a bike club the moment she'd passed her test her outrage had increased, but, as with the job with Port Health, it had been an occasion when Chloe refused to be manipulated, and the Honda had become her most cherished possession.

Thinking of it now made her long to feel the cool night air on her face, cruising out of the rush-hour traffic into Cheshire's leafy lanes, so while her mother was showering Chloe changed out of the formal clothes she'd worn for the interview, and with trousers and a thick sweater beneath her leathers, and a helmet on her short fair mop, she went down to the garage at street level.

Chloe's feelings at the end of her first day with Port Health were a mixture of satisfaction and disappointment. The satisfaction came from not having bungled anything. It also came from realising she'd retained some of the knowledge she'd picked up the previous year, while based at the port for a couple of weeks as a student, and from having made, under the supervision of James Hanbury, the chief port health officer, her first inspection of a ship.

It was a Dutch tanker that had come in on the first tide of her first day, and they had boarded it together. Her superior was a charming elderly man who was only too happy to expound to her with great fluency and accuracy the functions of Port Health, and Chloe was happy to be renewing the acquaintance she'd made on her previous visit.

Her disappointment had come from discovering that they would be working together for only two weeks. 'I'm afraid that you and I are going to be ships that pass in the night, so to speak, Chloe,' he'd told her with an apologetic smile as they'd made their way to the captain's cabin. 'I'm taking early retirement, and am leaving at the end of next week.'

She had gazed at him with concerned hazel eyes.

'You're not ill, are you?'

James had laughed and said, 'No, not ill, just tired. I love the job, but I've been at it a long time and I'm ready for a rest.'

Her mind had started to whirl. She liked James Hanbury, liked him a lot. He didn't make her feel nervous, and he'd welcomed her into his department with genuine warmth. The thought of working under a new chief within a couple of weeks of starting with Port Health was daunting to say the least.

'Who will be taking your place?' she'd asked in dismay.

'It's no one you know,' he'd told her. 'No one that I know, for that matter. I believe his name is Thomas Saracen. He was previously a master mariner, but gave up the sea for some reason, and has completed the necessary training to make him eligible for this job.'

Chloe had gazed at him in surprise.

'A sea captain? And he's becoming a port health officer?'

'Chief port health officer,' he'd reminded her with a smile, 'and it's not all that unusual. Quite a lot of the fellows doing this sort of job have been ship's captains.'

As he'd explained the procedure for inspecting a ship for infestation, adequate arrangements for the preparation of food, and good sanitation, it had taken Chloe all her time to concentrate. She'd been visualising a burly bearded man sitting behind the desk in James's office, drinking rum and chewing tobacco, and the flight of fancy had been a lot easier to believe than the one she'd had about her mother.

The Dutch captain had produced a de-ratting certificate, so there had been no call to check for rat droppings or signs of their presence along the pipes and in the engine-rooms where they were sometimes attracted by the grease. The ship had been clean and in good condition, and her forebodings about the new chief had been shelved when the captain offered them lunch.

It had been an enjoyable meal, and as she had eaten Chloe had ignored the interest that her presence was arousing among the tanker's crew. That was something she would have to get used to—the fact that they hadn't seen a woman in weeks, sometimes months— but she'd thought with wry humour that a small plain girl in hard hat and waterproofs was a far cry from the dance of the seven veils and, that being so, she should be quite safe.

And with regard to this man of the sea, who was soon going to be featuring largely in her working life, Chloe comforted herself with the thought that in a way they would both be starting off on the same footing, both of them newcomers to the port.

* * *

On the Monday morning of Chloe's third week with Port Health the mild spring weather that had prevailed over recent days was missing. Grey skies hung overhead, and a chill wind stung her face as she pointed the Fireblade in the direction of Port House, the centre of health administration for the Ship Canal and the twenty-five miles of the River Weaver branching off it.

James Hanbury had explained to her during the short time they had worked together that, in years past, the Weaver had been a busy stretch of navigated water because of the salt trade, but now Port Health's interest in it was mainly connected with the occasional ship, barges, houseboats, and the pleasure steamers taking the sightseeing public along its length.

He had been helpful and informative, and now he'd gone. There had been a presentation from the authority and a special dinner in his honour, and then he'd taken his leave. Now his desk was empty of his trappings, and today the man who was to take his place would assume command.

As she parked the bike Chloe was aware that there was no strange car outside the offices as yet, but then it was only eight o'clock and their official starting time was not until half past. Hopefully there would be time for a coffee before he appeared, and a chat with Maureen Grant, the likeable mother of two teenage boys who dealt with the clerical side of Port Health.

The coffee was available, but not the chat. As Chloe went into the office, swinging her helmet from a slender wrist, Maureen said with a sympathetic smile, 'I'm afraid that it's a typical Monday morning, Chloe. There's a manifest here from the *Amperides*. She docked earlier, with pistachio nuts on board, and in view of the toxic problems that the Port of London and ourselves are having with nuts I think if James were here he would have wanted them inspected.'

'Have we got the certificates from the importer?' she asked.

'Yes, for once. All present and correct,' Maureen informed her.

'Right, then I'll get down there.' Chloe began to exchange the protective clothing she'd worn for the bike for the blue hard hat and yellow waterproof that was her outerwear on the port.

Chloe took a quick gulp of the coffee, her face serious. It would be cold on the dockside this morning, although that didn't bother her too much. She'd been out on the bike on colder days than this, but it would be her first venture into inspecting imported food on her own, and on top of that she would be missing when the Saracen man arrived.

She was turning to go when Maureen called her back. 'You're forgetting the lethal weapon,' she said with a grin, and, reaching up to a shelf beside Chloe's desk, she produced the sampling tool that Chloe would need for the task ahead. It was a cylindrical instrument about a foot long, tapering to a fine point, that would do the least amount of damage when inserted into the packaging of the goods.

It *was* cold on the dockside. Today the Mersey, lying loverlike beside the canal, and stretching as far as the eye could see, was bereft of Mediterranean tints. It looked grey and forbidding, and as one of the stevedores prised open the cargo to enable her to carry out the inspection Chloe knew it was going to be a long chilly day.

By late morning she found herself alone, working slowly and methodically through the delivery of nuts in drizzling rain. As the samples fell out of the sack into a small scoop that she was holding she emptied them into a plastic bag for testing. Engrossed in her task, she swivelled round, startled, dropping the bag in the process, as a deep voice said from behind, 'So this is where you're hiding. I'm sure I don't need to point out that scattering the nuts all over the place isn't going to speed their arrival with the public analysts.'

He wasn't in uniform like herself. His dark suit, white shirt and sober tie made her feel clumsy in her protective clothing, and with regard to his comments it seemed to have escaped him that it was his creeping up on her that had made her drop the bag.

'I'm not hiding,' she said distantly. 'I'm working. . . and I dropped the bag because you startled me. As to my being down here, would you rather I'd stayed in the office waiting to drop my curtsey instead of doing what I'm paid for?' she went on recklessly, feeling needled and off balance.

He didn't answer, just looked her over speculatively, as if *she* were some sort of doubtful cargo. Chloe eyed him back. Some sort of introduction this was turning out to be! Here was no heavyweight with a beard, indulging in rum and tobacco. He was tall and trim, without an ounce of spare flesh on him. His hair was dark and it fell in crisp glossy waves. His mouth was straight and unsmiling, and she thought he looked more like a bank manager than an ex-master mariner, but there were the eyes, keen, vigilant, as blue as the sea beneath a summer sky. . .sailor's eyes. As they met her own clear hazel gaze he held out a big brown hand and broke the silence.

'Tom Saracen,' he said briefly.

'Chloe Cavendish,' she replied with equal parsimony of speech.

'I'm told you're new here,' he said, bending effortlessly to scoop up the nuts.

'Yes. I've only been with Port Health for a fortnight.'

'Mmm. I see. Dangerous occupation for a woman.'

Chloe stiffened. This was good! Not only did he appear to be a much more arrogant specimen than the departed James, but the man was a chauvinist to boot!

'I believe that there are more than twenty women working in Port Health,' she said stiffly, 'and in any case I've always wanted a job like this.'

He held up his hand as if to ward her off.

'All right. You don't have to start quoting statistics to me. I am fully aware of the fact, and was merely commenting.'

Oh, *were* you, she thought angrily, and where were you when they were dishing out the tact?

'What training have you had?' he was asking.

'Careerwise. . .or on the port?'

'Here.'

'I've spent two weeks under James Hanbury's supervision. . .and enjoyed it immensely,' she couldn't resist adding.

'I see.' He pointed to the sacks of nuts. 'And you consider yourself competent enough to deal with this lot?'

'Yes, up to a point,' she told him evenly. 'As there

was no one else to do it, I came down here as soon as I arrived.'

He was frowning. 'Yes, of course. I had intended being here bright and early myself, but today of all days a domestic matter thrust itself in the way.'

Chloe was cold and wet, and she didn't really care about what might be going on in Tom Saracen's private life. For heaven's sake, they'd only met five minutes ago! Yet she couldn't stop herself from imagining him having breakfast in a gleaming kitchen, with an attractive family clustered around him as in the cereal adverts. Maybe that had been the problem, she thought with an impish smile. . .they'd run out of cornflakes!

'You're aware of how many kilos you have to send for testing?' he asked crisply.

'Yes, but I'm only halfway through as yet,' she explained.

Thomas Saracen looked up at the leaden sky and said with a shrug, 'Well, at least you're not getting soaked like myself. I'm going back to the office. I'd like a chat when you've finished.'

As he strode off, tall, straight and businesslike, Chloe hoped that it might be on a friendlier note than the one they'd just had, but she wasn't going to bank on it.

When lunchtime came she went back to the Port House to warm up some soup in the kitchen. The new chief officer was deep in conversation with Maureen as she squelched past the office door. He looked up but made no comment, neither did he intrude while she was eating, and when she left the cosy warmth of the kitchen, *en route* for the dockside again, he was deep in conversation on the telephone.

'That's lovely, sweetheart. Who's a clever girl?' she heard him say, and as she went down the stairs Chloe was smiling. That would be the glamorous wife reporting that she'd remembered to get the cornflakes. Did she have to say 'Permission to speak, Cap'n'? Chloe wondered. Having made his brief acquaintance, it was possible.

As she carried on testing the nuts Chloe was trying to adjust to what little she'd seen of her new boss. Physically he was quite something. There were a couple of dishy guys in the bike club, but they weren't in Saracen's league. Personality-wise she didn't think she was going to like him. There'd been no 'Pleased to meet you', or 'I hope we're going to work well together', just a staccato introduction and a hint of underlying criticism. . .and she hadn't even done anything wrong! James Hanbury's geniality, which hadn't decreased his efficiency, had been delightful, but in his place it looked as if she was going to be handed with a surly bossy boots.

It was the middle of the afternoon before she'd finished, and the moment she set foot in her office Thomas Saracen was behind her. 'We'll have that chat when you're ready,' he said. Restraining the urge to ask if it would be all right if she took off her wet clothes first, Chloe nodded without speaking.

When she went into his room he was seated sideways behind the desk, his gaze on the canal, with the Mersey beyond, and while he kept her standing there she had the strangest feeling of expectancy, as if the moment was going to be memorable, but it was dispelled as he swung round to face her and, pointing to a chair, said,

'I'm told that the urban street tiger on the parking lot belongs to you.'

'Yes, it does,' she said, unable to keep the amazement out of her voice. This man was a surprise a minute!

'Very striking,' he commented drily.

'*I* think so,' she told him with quiet pride, while wondering what sort of vehicle *he* drove. It was bound to be something solid and substantial, but they were supposed to be discussing the job. . .weren't they?

The same thought was obviously in Saracen's mind as he said briskly, 'Right, Chloe, let's get down to brass tacks. We're both new to the Port of Manchester, so we have that in common, but it ends there. The difference between us is that you know nothing. . .and I know plenty.'

Thanks a bunch, she thought grimly.

'That being so, I shall see to it that you are instructed in every part of the job.'

'I *have* spent some time here as a student,' she pointed out, nettled at his assumption of her ignorance, but he carried on as if she hadn't spoken.

'Obviously we can't work together all the time. Certain tasks you will have to perform on your own, but every spare moment I have I will spend with you.'

She stifled a groan. That might be all very well from the job point of view, but she had a feeling it wouldn't do much for her self-esteem. . .or peace of mind!

'I was previously deputy chief health officer at a southern port, and I've spent the last few days moving house,' he informed her crisply.

'Where to?' she asked without thinking.

He was smiling. . .for the first time. 'I've bought an

old stone house in Eastham. I can see the Ship Canal from the upper windows.'

Chloe felt a stab of envy. So the Saracen and his family wouldn't be cooped up in a high-rise flat, luxurious though it was, with a thousand roofs and chimneys for company.

'Are your family happy about the move?' she asked with polite curiosity, banishing her imaginings of the idyllic breakfast scene from her mind, while not forgetting his indulgent tone during the telephone conversation.

His face closed up and she wondered why. It had been a harmless enough question. The keen eyes weighed her up, and then he said, 'Yes, happy enough,' and, as if not wanting her to have the chance to take him up on it he said, 'I take it that *you're* a free agent?'

Chloe's thoughts went to Mike, who had a BMW K100, and always made a beeline for her when she went to the club, and rode as near to her as he could when the gang of them were on the road. He was attractive and uncomplicated, with the same pale gold fairness as herself, and she'd thought that maybe one day. . .

And then in a different dimension there was her mother, pleasure-loving, extravagant, who was quick to demand her presence even though Chloe pleased her so little. But that wasn't what he meant, was it?

'I'm unattached, if that's what you mean,' she told him, and wondered why the pronouncement didn't sound as satisfying as it usually did.

He was ready to change the subject.

'Have you been making sure that all incoming ships'

crews have seen the HIV video that Port Health have brought out?' he wanted to know.

Chloe nodded. 'Yes. We've been taking it on board, leaving it for a couple of hours to give the captains a chance to show it to their crew, and then calling back for it before the ships have sailed, and along with that we've been issuing them with the leaflet that goes with it.'

'Good,' he said briskly. 'It is an amazing thought in this day and age that some of the crews from African ships and such like haven't even heard of Aids. Keeping *that* scourge away from the seafaring population, and the general public that they might be involved with, is just as important a part of our job as making sure that those on board ship have safe drinking water.'

He got to his feet. 'Tomorrow I intend to familiarise myself with all the docks—Runcorn, Ellesmere Port, Stanlow and the rest. I need to get the feel of the place, and see no reason why you shouldn't come along, just as long as we get no more iffy nuts, or a rush of ships that are due for inspection. On the subject of nuts, what was the final outcome on your day's labours?'

'I kept one sack back just to be sure. The result from the public analyst should be back within forty-eight hours. The others have been released.'

He nodded, and she would have liked to know if it was in approval or merely a reflex action.

'Have you been called out since you came to Port Health?' he asked as he shuffled together the papers on his desk and deposited them in a leather briefcase.

'No,' she told him, 'but James Hanbury warned me

that we take turns at being on twenty-four-hour call-out.'

'Yes, well, I'll take the first week,' he said. 'I may not have an urban street tiger at my disposal, but my old Rover will get me where I want to go with reasonable speed should there be an emergency.'

'Yes, of course,' she murmured, adjusting to the thought of spending a full day under the wing of this rather abrasive newcomer. It wasn't a prospect to relish. As he'd pointed out, *she* knew nothing, while *he* knew it all! However, one thing was for sure: she was going to have to get used to it. . .working with him, as, after all, Thomas Saracen, Maureen and herself *were* Port Health. They were committed to keeping the environment healthy, just as much as doctors and their counterparts were involved with the individual.

When Chloe set off for home the rain had cleared, and the early evening sky was full of stars. For some reason that she didn't understand she ignored the route to Manchester and took a detour around the pretty little village of Eastham, and as she zoomed past the houses, with lights on behind drawn curtains, she wondered which one belonged to Tom Saracen and the 'clever girl'.

CHAPTER TWO

NEXT day at the Port House Chloe found that Tom Saracen had discarded the dark suit for Port Health uniform, and in a crisp white shirt with four gold flashes on the shoulder, and dark trousers, he looked more official than the previous day, and yet, for some reason that she couldn't fathom, less forbidding.

'Why four?' she asked curiously when he called her into his office where he was glancing over a manifest lying on the desk.

'What?' he asked absently.

'Why four pips on your shoulder?'

Her own white shirt had two, and on James Hanbury's there had been three.

'Oh, that. The extra one is to denote that I've been a ship's captain.'

'I see.'

He was eyeing the clear blue sky through the window that overlooked the canal, and as she watched him Chloe was thinking that wherever they went today she would feel less at a disadvantage, as they would both be dressed the same, and doing the same thing, except for the fact that he'd been so quick to point out. . .*her* knowledge was nil, while *his* was boundless!

She wasn't in complete agreement about that at all. She'd done a fortnight's training on the port last summer, and hadn't forgotten anything she'd learnt, and she'd just spent two weeks with James. Did

Saracen think she went about with her eyes closed and her ears blocked? During a restless night she had vowed that she was going to make herself so indispensable that he would end up grovelling at her feet, and she had ended up laughing in the darkness at the remoteness of such a prospect.

Nevertheless she was determined to show her abilities. She'd had no problems with the degree course, and was contemplating further studies. Her mind was quick, she wasn't afraid of hard work, and the bonus was that she would be doing it beside the waterway that she'd never forgotten since the days when she'd played beside it outside her father's business premises.

'We'll start at this end, I think,' he said, getting to his feet, and as he took down his hat and outdoor coat off the peg Chloe saw that his gaze had transferred itself to the Runcorn Bridge, its graceful span dominating the skyline.

'It's the third largest of its type in the world,' she told him, 'built in 1963 to replace the old transporter bridge.'

'Yes, I know,' he said slowly, and she thought *he* would! Was she going to have to dedicate the rest of her days to finding something he *didn't* know?

There was no likelihood of that occurring as they stood by the locks and the big square dock at the beginning of the ship canal. They had just left the building that housed the harbourmaster and port control, and now Tom Saracen was chatting in a lucid and precise manner with the lockmaster. She'd watched as he'd introduced himself to the port officials, and had admitted to herself that this dark, rather taciturn man knew what it was all about. He was obviously fully informed about all aspects of port health, and grasped any point under discussion in a way that had those in his company eyeing him with wary respect.

Maybe he wasn't such a pain after all, Chloe thought, but she still had reservations, and she felt as if she needed to get her eyes fixed on something other than Tom Saracen for a while. She looked around her. Across the wide expanse of the Mersey she could see the tall buildings of Liverpool, with the outline of the cathedral standing out among them, and nearer, lying beside her in the lock, was a brightly painted push-tug, waiting to live up to its name by propelling two empty barges that had just been relieved of their liquid cargos out into open water. They were positioned in front of it, and when the lock gates opened they would sail through to Seaforth, past where a red buoy marked the end of Port Health jurisdiction.

There were two tankers in the dock. They'd been on the list of arrivals that came with every tide from port control, and she'd noted that there was no cause to board them as they docked regularly at the port, and were in possession of current de-ratting certificates.

On land behind the docks were the tank farms for oil and chemicals. Hardly a romantic scene, but it was a vision of the trading and commerce that took place on the famous waterway, and *she* was a part of it.

A long time ago a man of vision and foresight called Daniel Adamson had gathered together businessmen and local dignitaries, and the idea of the Ship Canal had been born. Sadly he hadn't lived to see the day of its opening, but, as proof of the supreme common sense of his dream, it was still functioning a hundred years on.

There had been times in the past, particularly after losing her father, when Chloe had felt as if she was going nowhere, and had known that her mother was happy for it to be so, but not now. She'd got herself an interesting and challenging job, that wasn't all going to be checking nuts for toxic substances—far from it—and it was in surroundings that interested her greatly. At last her mother had been made to accept that her daughter wasn't going to become a clone of herself.

She was twenty-eight years old, and a free agent. She'd confirmed that fact with her new boss, though why he'd asked the question she really didn't know. He'd already commented that the job was dangerous, so perhaps he'd been checking to see if she had a husband or a young family. Though lots of women with families took risky jobs, just the same as men, if they were to survive financially, and at the same time prove their worth. Tom Saracen needn't have concerned himself. She *was* unattached, and as she eyed the tall perfectionist, chatting easily to the lockmaster, Chloe couldn't help wondering what manner of woman had put the fetters around *him*.

She glanced across and saw that the deputy harbourmaster was leaving the control building and moving towards them. When he drew level he said, 'We've just had a call from the *Sondheim*, a Danish transporter of 8,000 tonnes. She's radioed in to say that she'll be berthing within the hour and has a sick crewman on board. I've phoned the doc. He'll meet you here in fifteen minutes.'

Tom Saracen nodded. 'Fine. Where's she been?'

'African coast,' the other man informed him laconically.

When he'd gone Chloe said, 'So what happens now?'

'We wait for the port health medical officer. Normally *we* would have contacted him, but control have done it for us, seeing that we're here instead of in the office. When he arrives we go on board with him to evaluate the situation. We would have been boarding her in any case as the *Sondheim* was on today's list of ships that have been to ports where infectious diseases are rife.

'The port medical officer doesn't play as big a part in port health as we do, but these are the occasions when we require his presence. *Our* function in the event of something highly infectious is to prevent it from spreading among the rest of the crew, and through them on to the mainland.'

As a car appeared at the other side of the lock Tom said, 'That looks like Martin Page, the medical officer, now,' and, swivelling back to face the canal, 'and here comes the *Sondheim*.'

'If she's been to Africa, it could be anything,' the elderly medical officer said gloomily as they waited for the ship to come alongside, 'and we'll soon know. Thank God it's not like the old days when ships used to come in with half the crew suffering from smallpox, and the canal boats had children on board dying from diptheria and suchlike.' He turned to Chloe and asked with a dry chuckle, 'How would you have liked being a port health officer in those conditions, young lady?'

She smiled back. 'I think I'd have been happier serving behind the counter in Woolworths.'

Tom Saracen was watching her and from the glint in

his eye she felt that perhaps that was where he thought she *should* be.

When they went on board, the Danish captain explained in good English that the first mate, an overweight man in his forties, had been ill over the past few days with intense pain in the stomach and between the shoulder-blades, and had also been vomiting.

'Has he had all his vaccinations?' Martin Page asked, and was informed that he had. 'Any fever?' he queried as he examined the man's stomach and between the shoulder-blades.

The man shook his head. 'Naw, just this awful pain, Doc.'

Martin Page felt at his neck glands, looked down his throat, checked his ears, and then probed gently in the groin. When at last he straightened up he told the captain, 'Can't put my finger on it with just this brief examination, but I don't think it's anything he's picked up in the tropics. My guess would be a gallstone stuck in the bile duct. I'll have him admitted to hospital for tests. If it *is* gallstones, ultrasound scanning will show it up.'

Chloe's face had dropped and Tom Saracen murmured drily in her ear, 'What's the matter? Were you expecting nothing less than the plague or Lassa fever? This fellow looks as if he's been around long enough to have developed his own immunity to those sort of infections.'

She *had* been expecting something a bit more exciting, but she could hardly tell him *that*, with the poor man on the bunk in agony.

'There is always a chance I'm wrong. The ship *has*

been to Africa, so don't take any chances. I would do your usual routine,' the medical officer advised.

Saracen nodded as they all proceeded to the deck above. 'Of course. I couldn't agree more. I'll issue the forms for any member of the crew who wants to go ashore, but will postpone any fumigation or disinfection until we know what ails the fellow.'

He turned to Chloe. '*You* can deal with that, Chloe. It's a form in three parts that has to be issued and given to those concerned. The on-shore crew member keeps one part of it to give to his GP in the event of him becoming ill, a second is sent to the medical officer of health in the area, and the third *we* keep. OK?'

'Yes,' she said briefly.

When she went back downstairs to the captain's cabin he informed her that three men wanted to go on shore, and by the time she'd dealt with the paperwork the ambulance had put in a speedy appearance, and the sick bosun was being stretchered carefully into it.

As she made her way back up the narrow steps that led to the deck she heard Martin Page say, 'How's she settling in?'

Chloe stopped with her foot poised between the steps.

'So-so,' Tom Saracen replied. 'But you know what young girls are like. . .think they know it all, and it takes some swallowing. No doubt we'll get there in the end, but there *are* moments when I feel that I'd have been happier with a different arrangement.'

She felt her blood heat. How dared he discuss her like that? As if she were some sort of young bimbo. She hadn't been wrong. He resented the fact that he'd got a female assistant. They'd only met yesterday and he'd already written her off as useless before he'd even seen her in action! Well! She would show him! He might look like a Greek god, but he was a mindless oaf, and she flew up the rest of the stairway with a speed that catapulted her on to the deck like a jack-in-the-box.

Saracen eyed her flaming cheeks and said, 'You look hot. Is it the heat of the captain's cabin, or are *you* going down with something?'

He'd like that, she thought furiously, proof of her female frailty, and an excuse to get her from under his feet.

'No, I am not,' she said with cold politeness.

He stared at her. The drop in temperature in her voice was at odds with the high colour, but he didn't comment further, just said evenly, 'Right, we'll get on our way, then. See you again no doubt, Martin.' And he preceded her down the gangplank.

When they stood together on the dockside once more he said, 'What are you doing about lunch? It's gone twelve.'

'I've left a sandwich in the kitchen,' she said stiffly.

'I'll run you back, then,' he offered, 'but I want to call at the house for a moment on the way. Do you mind?'

'No, of course not,' she told him in the same frigid tone. She had weightier things than that to get peeved about. . .and she was curious to see his domestic set-up.

As he drove towards the village Chloe's determination to treat him with silent disdain went by the board, and after he'd glanced at her set face a couple of times she said angrily, 'I'm twenty-eight!'

Saracen gazed at her blankly.

'Almost as old as you!' she persisted.

He gave a dry laugh. 'Hardly. I can give you ten years, *and* a couple more, but I'm not with you. Am I supposed to deduce something from that statement?'

'I'm twenty-eight!' she repeated, aware that her voice was rising, and her outrage showing through. 'Not a silly young girl!'

'My goodness! Somebody's been treading on *your* toes!' he exclaimed as he negotiated a sharp right turn that took them off the main road. 'Was it one of the guys on board getting fresh? I'm afraid *that* isn't one of the perks of the job, unless you like that sort of thing. If you don't, you have to remember that they've been cooped up for weeks without any female company.'

Chloe thought she would explode with rage. He was heaping the insults on. Implying that she might fancy a romp with a randy sailor, and, if she didn't, warning her that the poor souls weren't to blame if they did go off the rails!

'It *was* someone on the *Sondheim* who upset me, yes,' she told him, on a collision course now, and not caring a damn if she *did* antagonise her boss. *He* wasn't behind the door when it was the other way round. . .was he?

His face had tightened.

'Who?'

'You!'

'Me?'

'I heard you discussing me with the medical officer.'

His expression was slack now. . .with amazement, but he was turning on to a short drive that led to a sprawling converted barn, and it looked as if the conversation would have to be shelved for the moment.

'We'll finish that discussion later,' he promised grimly. 'In the meantime, let me introduce you to my family.'

Chloe didn't move. She'd changed her mind. She didn't want to meet the wife and kids from the imaginary kitchen scene now, and she didn't know why. Maybe it was because he irritated her so much. . .and maybe it wasn't. Perhaps it was because she wasn't too hot on family life. . .not in recent years anyway.

He was waiting for her to get out of the car and it would be rude not to do so, so she eased herself out and stood beside him on the path, a slender figure in a dark skirt and the white shirt with its gold braid on the shoulder.

As she looked around her the wind lifted her hair and whipped the skirt against her legs, and as she bent to straighten it a voice said from near by, 'Tom! We weren't expecting you until this evening.'

It wasn't a young voice. The woman who stood in the open doorway was old. She was small and dainty with white hair, and a caliper on her leg.

'Hi, Mum,' he said, and the warmth in his voice was that of a deep affection. 'Where's Lucy?'

'Round the back doing some weeding,' she said.

'Really?' he echoed disbelievingly.

'Yes, really,' she told him with a quizzical smile. 'We're adjusting with every second.'

His face was sombre. 'I hope you're right.' Then, as if throwing a burden off his shoulders, he said, 'I'd like you to meet my assistant. . .Chloe Cavendish.'

The white-haired woman held out a thin hand. 'How do you do, my dear? I'm Grace Saracen, Tom's mother, and, if I'm not mistaken, here comes the rest of the family.'

Chloe followed her gaze and saw a teenage girl come round the side of the house. Her eyes widened. This was the rest of his family? Where was the focal point. . .the mother?

The girl had Saracen's dark colouring and vivid blue eyes. . .and his determined chin, but she didn't appear to have inherited his zest. She leant against the fence and eyed them sulkily from a distance.

When he said briskly, 'Say hello to Chloe, Lucy,' she mumbled a surly greeting, and Chloe saw him flinch. She wondered if his daughter's lack of enthusiasm was the cause of it, or something deeper. When he turned to his mother and said, 'I'll pop back for a bite, Mum, when I've dropped Chloe off,' she had a feeling that he was coming back to check up on them.

He was silent as they drove out of the village, and, having got over her earlier annoyance, Chloe would have liked to talk, but his withdrawn expression was off-putting to say the least. In the end it was he who broke the silence, and it was clear that his domestic problems hadn't pushed their earlier conversation out of his mind.

'And so what did I do on board the *Sondheim* that caused your hackles to rise to such an extent?' he asked drily.

'You were discussing me with the medical officer, and I didn't like your comments!'

His dark brows rose. 'I don't recall doing that. The only conversation I had with Martin Page, apart from

Port Health matters, was about my daughter, Lucy, the young lady who has just greeted you so graciously.' His voice toughened as he went on to say, 'I am not in the habit of discussing my staff with anyone. If at any time in the future I have any complaints regarding yourself, you will be the first and only person to hear about them.'

Chloe felt her cheeks start to burn. The 'young girl' being discussed was his daughter. . .not his assistant! She'd made a first-class fool of herself. It was going from bad to worse between them. Some start for a good working relationship!

'I knew Martin Page years ago, when I was first married, and we worked together some time back when we were both based down south,' he was explaining flatly. 'That was why he was enquiring about Lucy.' His voice had lost its vibrancy. 'You see, *he* knows about what happened to my wife.'

It was poking her nose into his affairs, but he *had* brought up the subject, and she *had* to ask. She'd just met Saracen's mother and daughter, and that had been it, and, from what the old lady had said, it *was* it.

'And what was that?' she probed.

'Herta was Dutch. I met her in Rotterdam when I was a master mariner. I was captain of a ship belonging to her father. . .and so was she.'

Chloe gaped at him.

'Your wife was a master mariner?'

'Yes. We both had our own ships. When Lucy was born I wanted her to give it up, but she loved the life too much—the freedom, the ever-changing scene— and so my mother cared for Lucy while we were away.'

'You must have seen very little of each other!' she

said in continuing amazement. 'The separation when just the husband is at sea must be bad enough, but both of you. . .!'

His voice was bitter as he said, 'Herta had already made a stand for equal rights for women with the career she'd chosen, and in the end it was *I* who gave up the sea. I couldn't stand Lucy being separated from *both* of us. It was another victory for the fair sex. . .if fair is the right word.'

Chloe had been listening open mouthed, and when he'd finished speaking it was the obvious question that stumbled forth.

'And where is she now?'

'Dead,' he said harshly. 'A collision on a dark night in atrocious weather. To coin a familiar phrase, she went down with her ship.'

'Oh! How dreadful!' she breathed. 'And you were left to look after Lucy?'

His smile when it came was less bitter than his voice had been. 'I was already doing that with my mother's help. We had adjustments to make, of course, when Herta was lost, but Lucy was doing fine until we moved up here last week. I know that it's a difficult age for a child who has already known trauma in her life to be uprooted, but at the time it seemed the right thing to do. I'd been headhunted for the job, and when I asked her if she'd like to come up north she was really keen. However, since we arrived, I'm not sure.

'Mother is convinced that she'll be all right when she starts at her new school after Easter, as she's a good mixer usually. With it being only a couple of weeks off we thought it better if she started at the beginning of the new term, rather than breaking the ice and then being off again almost immediately, but at the moment she's moping around like a lost soul.'

'Poor lamb,' Chloe said softly. 'How old is she?'

'Thirteen.'

'That was roughly my age when my dad died. I thought I'd never smile again. He had a business on the Ship Canal, and every spare minute I had I was round there. When he went my mother sold it, and now she spends her time squandering his money, and trying to fashion *me* into the same mould as herself.' Her smile was wry. 'But she hasn't managed it so far.'

He laughed. 'I can believe that. A job in Port Health and an urban street tiger don't exactly sound like the trappings of a débutante. You've obviously got a mind of your own.'

'Most of the time I give in to her for the sake of peace,' she told him, unaware that her voice was wistful, 'but on some things, like the ones you've just mentioned, I was immovable.'

'Good for you, but do remember that the job *can* be dangerous.'

'Not as dangerous as that of a ship's captain when the sea turns vicious.'

The words had spilled out before she had time to think, and if she could have bitten them back she would have.

'Hopefully not,' he said grimly, and swished to a halt outside Port House.

Chloe ate her lunch without it registering. She was stunned by the morning's revelations, her thoughts leaping from one thing to another. It was incredible to think that Tom Saracen's wife had been a sea captain, and even harder to believe that it had meant more to her than her child. What about the Dutch grandparents? Where did they fit into the scheme of things? Had they been supportive of their daughter's going back to sea after her child was born? And what had they thought of their son-in-law giving it up for Lucy's sake?

She understood now why he wasn't exactly a bundle of fun. It was some raw deal he'd had in the marriage stakes, and consequently his opinion of her own sex wasn't very high. His wife must have been some woman, though, and yet didn't most women captain a ship. . .a ship called 'home and family'? Sometimes it was just as demanding a job. . .*and* requiring special skills.

It amazed her to think that Tom had given up his job, rather than his wife hers, and she had to admire him for it. It would seem that there'd been three females in his life—his wife, his daughter. . .and his ship, and he'd steered to where the need was greatest.

She'd been curious about his family from the moment of their meeting the previous day—why, she didn't know. Now she'd been put in the picture. Had he deliberately taken her to the house to show her that his life wasn't a bed of roses? Hardly. He barely knew her and, in any case, Tom Saracen was too controlled, too self-contained to do that.

He might have had a raw deal, but it was clear that he had support from his mother, that they had a loving relationship, and Chloe felt tears rise in her throat as she thought of the lack of rapport between her mother and herself.

And what about herself? Flying off the handle over
something that didn't concern her. He must have
thought her a neurotic idiot, and then, after listening
to the traumas of *his* life, she had to go burbling on
about her own family disadvantages. Talk about bringing it all out into the open!

As she washed her dishes Chloe wondered if she
could take Lucy to a pop concert or something similar.
Sometimes teenagers found it easier to communicate
with a stranger than their parents.

When Tom Saracen came back after lunch she put
the suggestion to him, knowing that if she allowed
herself time to think she might have doubts about
becoming involved in his affairs.

His eyes widened in surprise, and for a moment she
saw behind his mask of competency. 'I think she'd like
that very much,' he said quickly. 'Until Lucy starts
school young female company is going to be in short
supply.' The corners of his mouth lifted. 'I use the
term "young" with care, bearing in mind that you *are*
twenty-eight.'

Chloe flushed to the pale gold roots of her hair. She
didn't want to be reminded of her humiliating mistake
of the morning, certainly not with amusement, and so,
gathering her dignity together, she said, 'I'm not free
this evening, but there are a couple of groups on at
one of the theatres in Manchester on Friday night. Is
she into pop?'

He groaned. 'She certainly is. I've got aching ear-
drums to prove it! I'll put the suggestion to her as soon
as I get in. . .and thanks.'

'My pleasure,' she said lightly, and wondered if it
would be. It certainly wouldn't if *he* chose to come,

and in a panic she said, 'Just the two of us—er—girls' night out.'

'Yes, of course,' he agreed, back to his usual clipped impersonality. '*I've* got plenty to do. Twenty-four hours in the day isn't long enough when one has just moved house.'

As she wove the bike in and out of the motorway traffic on the way home her mind was still occupied with Tom Saracen and his affairs, and Chloe decided that, given his attractions, and the fact that he was unattached, the average woman would be prepared to ignore his abrupt manner, or, alternatively, vow to mellow him, if he would look her way. That being so, there was certain to be someone he turned to for his needs. It was so with most men.

When she got home there was a note from her mother to say she'd gone to see *Phantom of the Opera*. . .for the fourth time. . .and Chloe could either eat out or make herself a sandwich. She would be eating out, she thought, with a smile of anticipation. It was the monthly meeting of the motorcycle club. A gang of them, all Honda owners, congregated at the Bluebell, a pub in a Manchester suburb that was clean and cosy with a biker-friendly landlord. Tonight the organising of two practice runs and a vote on how many were in favour of going to the Isle of Man for the Junior TT were the main items on the agenda.

They were all gathered in a small room at the back, and when Chloe arrived Mike Standish moved along the seat so that she could sit beside him. The two of them were good friends with regards to the club, but so far hadn't spent any time together in any other social context, though she sensed that it wasn't going to be long before Mike asked her out. She liked him, and saw no reason not to accept if the invitation should be forthcoming, but as they exchanged greetings she realised how boyish and immature he looked, and wondered why she'd never noticed it before.

'How's the new job going?' he asked, as she'd told him she was starting with Port Health at the previous meeting.

'Fine,' she told him with a smile. 'The only snag is that my boss is new, too, and is a bit of a. . .'

Her voice had petered out at the end of the sentence as she'd asked herself why on earth she'd had to bring Tom Saracen into the conversation. He'd been on her mind enough the last two days; it was time she got him in perspective.

'Pain?' Mike was asking with a grin, and she found herself smiling back.

'Not so much a pain as a potion,' she replied, and the subject was dropped.

When Mike drew her away from the others later in the evening, and draped his arm across her shoulders, Chloe guessed that tonight was going to be the night. He was going to ask her out, and when he spoke she knew she was right.

'Can I take you out somewhere, Chloe?' he asked. 'I don't mean on the bikes. . .for a meal or something?'

When she didn't answer he said, 'We get on well, don't we, and I'd like it to be more; what do you say?'

What could she say? That she'd been comparing him with an older man for some reason, and it had made him seem gauche. That wouldn't be fair, would it, and

Mike would take a dim view of the comparison. He was an easy-going sort of guy, but she was pretty sure *that* wouldn't go down too well. The truth of the matter was that *he* hadn't changed. . .*she* had, and the sooner she came back to reality, the better.

'Yes, I'd love to go out with you, Mike,' she told him with a wide smile, and was ninety per cent sure that she meant it.

CHAPTER THREE

THE following morning, as Chloe and Maureen were having a coffee before the day's duties commenced, Tom Saracen rang in. He sounded uptight and irritable and proceeded to explain why to Chloe.

'I've just had a call from the solicitors who're handling the sale of my house at the other end,' he said tersely. 'The purchasers should have been completing today, and at the last moment they've started dithering. We've exchanged contracts, so they can't very well renege on me, but my legal buff foresees problems. He's been in touch with their solicitor and got nowhere. Now he's suggesting that I go to see them personally, and it doesn't look as if I have much choice.

'I can't afford any delay. I've taken a bridging loan out so that we would be settled in at this end when I started the job, and I don't want that to go on indefinitely. So I'll be back as soon as I can, and in the meantime keep your fingers crossed that no problems arise.'

His voice lifted. 'I mentioned your offer to Lucy and she jumped at the chance, so when I get back, which I'm expecting to be late this evening, we'll sort something out, eh?'

'Yes, of course,' she agreed, 'and good luck with your negotiations.'

'Thanks. I think I might need it,' he said with a return to his previous tetchy tone.

'So?' Maureen said, eyeing her over her coffee-cup. 'What was all that about?'

Tom Saracen won't be in today. There are problems regarding his house sale. He's going down south to see if he can persuade the folks who are buying it to stick to the contract. It's to be hoped he won't have to rely on charm, because from what I've seen so far it's in short supply.'

Maureen eyed her in surprise.

'You're joking! That man is memorable. I can just see him steeering his ship in a rough sea with those incredible eyes raking the horizon.'

'So can I,' Chloe agreed laughingly, 'but what's that got to do with charm? He has a very poor opinion of our sex for one thing, so that doesn't exactly put him at the top of the charisma charts.'

'It won't please him being away from the job,' Maureen said on a more serious note. 'If ever I saw a man who likes the "i"s dotted, and the "t"s crossed, it's our new chief. He was going to put you through your paces today,' she added with a mischievous smile.

Chloe grimaced. 'You make me sound like a racehorse.'

'A young colt, perhaps?' the other woman suggested laughingly.

Chloe pulled a face again. 'I'd like to know what *he* sees me as!' She glanced at her watch. 'I'd better get cracking with what I'm paid to do, or he'll be labelling me useless.'

'Hardly!' Maureen protested. 'By the end of the

month Tom Saracen will have to watch his stripes. You'll be eating the job.'

'Or Saracen will be devouring *me*,' Chloe said with a theatrical shudder.

The print-out of arrivals on the morning tide was on Tom's desk, and as Chloe checked through it she was relieved to see that there were no doubtful ones on it. . .none that needed to be inspected. She'd done it once under James Hanbury's supervision, on her first day at the port, and now felt that she could cope if she had to, but there was no way she wanted to put a foot wrong with Tom Saracen. She would rather such functions were performed by him until she'd had a little more practice.

It was the duty of Port Health to board any ships that had gone six months or over without being inspected, the purpose being to make sure that cooking facilities, sanitation and refrigeration arrangements were satisfactory. It was also to ascertain that there was no infestation on board of such as rats or cockroaches. Once the port health officer was satisfied that there were no rodents on board, the captain would be issued with a de-ratting certificate, which had to be renewed every six months.

Another reason for boarding would be if a ship had stopped at any port listed as infectious by the World Health Organization in Geneva. Then it was the duty of Port Health to make sure that there was no unreported illness on board, or other signs of infection.

Thirdly, their presence would be required if a captain radioed that he was coming into port with some kind of emergency on board, such as a sick seaman, or problems with the drinking water.

On today's list there appeared to be no such problems—not on the first tide, anyway—and Chloe turned her attention to various messages coming through from the Port of London, which included a reminder that there were still continuing problems with cargoes of nuts.

An interruption came in the form of a message from port control to say that the *Porthos*, a Greek transporter ship, had radioed in to say they had an animal on board.

'Where are they now?' she asked.

'Inward bound for Stanlow,' was the reply.

'Right. I'll get down there,' she told them, and to Maureen, 'If anybody wants me I'll be on the *Porthos*. They've got an animal on board.'

'Do you know what to do?' the other woman asked.

'I think so. It's mainly a matter of explaining the rabies restrictions to the captain, and who knows, if I get it right I might get a pat on the head from his highness!'

It was the responsibility of Port Health to see that notices setting out the rules and regulations regarding rabies were clearly on view at salient points along the canal, and when they were notified that a ship had docked with an animal on board it was their duty to tell the captain that the animal must stay locked up all the time the ship was in the port. Any failure to do so that might result in its getting on to the mainland carried a heavy fine, and the ship's captain had to sign a form to the effect that he understood the seriousness of the matter.

It was a clear cold morning and a breeze from across the Mersey stung Chloe's cheeks as she pointed the bike towards the dock where the *Porthos* would shortly be coming alongside.

Today she was dressed in navy trousers and a chunky sweater of the same colour, with the regulation gold flashes on the shoulder, and with the bag that held all her equipment for the job swinging from her hand and the blue hard hat on her head she presented a picture of trim feminine efficiency as she boarded the ship some fifteen minutes later.

The Greek crew eyed her admiringly as she made her way to the captain's cabin and, remembering Tom Saracen's comments of the previous day, she wished them a restrained 'Good morning' and went on her way.

'I believe that you have an animal on board,' she said after she'd introduced herself to the elderly Greek captain.

'Yes, a dog,' he told her in reasonable English.

'Who does it belong to?' she asked.

'It ees mine. Zeus, he go everywhere wiz me.'

'May I see him, please?' she requested politely.

He led the way to a small cabin below decks, and when he unlocked the door a big black dog of mixed parentage leapt off the bunk, and would have romped past them if the captain hadn't grabbed its collar.

After he'd thrust it back inside and locked the door he led the way back to his office, and Chloe told him, 'Will you please see that the dog is secure, Captain? It could easily have escaped and been on the shore within seconds.'

'Yes. I will do that.' He shrugged narrow shoulders, and his eyes didn't meet hers as he went on to say, 'We have only just this minute docked at your port.'

'I'm aware of that,' she said pleasantly. 'But you must keep the animal tied up all the time you are here, because with regard to rabies protection in the United Kingdom you are required to keep any animal on board ship securely locked away while you are in port. It should not have access to anyone, apart from yourself for feeding purposes.'

She opened her bag. 'I have here a notice explaining the requirements regarding rabies protection, which I have to ask you to read and then sign, to show that you are aware of the conditions.'

His eyes flicked over it, and then he signed as requested. Once he had done so, Chloe asked, 'Have you a current de-ratting certificate?'

He nodded, and when he produced it she saw that it didn't need renewing for a couple of months, and so she departed, after leaving him with the HIV video and a supply of leaflets for the crew to read, and explaining that she would call back for the video before the ship sailed.

Travelling back to Port House, Chloe was satisfied with the way she'd dealt with that matter of Port Health routine, though it did occur to her that it wouldn't have been quite as straightforward if the dog had escaped. It would have been a serious offence and the captain would have had to face a penalty.

The rest of the day passed quickly enough, and when the time had come to go home there had been no further word from Tom Saracen, which was not surprising as he was hardly likely to be back yet.

It was eleven o'clock when the phone rang and her mother answered it. Lorraine had spent the evening in for once, watching TV and munching her favourite chocolates, and Chloe, curled up in bed with a thriller, was surprised when told the call was for her.

'It's your boss on the line,' Lorraine said with a rare show of interest. 'Why would he be ringing you at *this* time?'

'I'm sure I don't know,' Chloe told her as she picked up the extension by the bed.

'Chloe?'

As his voice came over the line it was even less amiable than during his first call of the day, and she immediately thought that the house sale had fallen through, but she was jumping to conclusions.

'I've just got back,' he said with steely precision, 'and I called in a pub by the docks for a drink and a bite before I went home.'

'Yes?' she said, wondering what all this was about. It was a bit late in the day for a blow-by-blow account of what he'd been up to, and was she interested?

'One of the fellows from port control was in there, and he recognised me and came across. He pointed out an oldish Greek man at the bar.'

'Yes?' she said again. This had to be leading some-where, she supposed.

'The port control chappie said that he was the captain of the *Porthos*, and that he'd got a dog outside.'

Chloe's insides did a somersault. It *was* leading somewhere, and she didn't think she wanted to know.

'As we observed him he went outside and called a big black mongrel to him that was wolfing down a meat pie in the beer garden. Need I go on?'

'No,' she said weakly.

'So what the dickens is going on, Chloe?' he gritted.

'As soon as I turn my back there is trouble. You were notified that the ship had an animal on board. It's simple enough to deliver the rabies warning, and make sure that the captain understands. Why didn't you do that?'

'I did,' she protested, her voice rising. 'And he understood!'

There was a moment's silence, and then he said, 'You'd better be sure about it. This is serious. The Greek captain is in big trouble. There will be a court case.'

'I went on board the *Porthos* and followed the routine set out for Port Health with regard to rabies,' she said quietly. 'He had the dog in a cabin and it wasn't tied up. I told him that it wasn't satisfactory and that it must be secure all the time he was in the port. He understood, all right, although I wouldn't have said he was bursting with enthusiasm at the idea.'

'You've got a signature from him?'

Chloe felt herself bristling. This man thought that nobody could do anything but himself!

'Yes, of course.'

She heard him sigh at the other end of the line, and wondered whether it was with relief, exasperation at having to rely on a wet-behind-the-ears graduate, or in weariness. Whatever it was, she felt that *she* could have done without being subjected to the third degree at this hour of the night!

'Right. I'll speak to you in the morning,' he said in a slightly calmer tone, and rang off.

Chloe flung herself back against the pillows, cheeks red, eyes stormy. She'd done one thing on her own and it had gone haywire, but she was blessed if she was going to let it get to her. She'd done her job as it was set out. The Greek captain had known the risk he was taking, that the rabies laws were fierce, but Saracen hadn't been exactly convinced that she wasn't to blame in some way or other. It would give her great pleasure to wave the man's signature under his nose in the morning, she thought angrily, but there was misery inside her, too. This wasn't how she'd planned her debut in Port Health, with a bossy doubting Thomas breathing down her neck.

When she got to Port House the next morning at eight o'clock Saracen's car was already parked outside, and Chloe groaned. She'd been hoping for a few moments to herself before they came face to face. . . maybe if she let herself in quietly. . .but the moment she set foot in the entrance hall he called her name.

When she went into his office he was seated behind the desk, and as she looked at him Chloe felt her heartbeats quickening, and it was difficult to breathe. She hadn't seen him since Tuesday, and the impact of his looks and presence was hitting her all over again. Tom Saracen really was a very striking man, and she felt her blood warm, but she wasn't here to admire him. She intended to make him see that she wasn't going to be intimidated.

'It's no good creeping past,' he said with his dry smile. 'You can't expect to arrive unannounced on the Fireblade.'

For a moment the irritation he aroused in her was forgotten, and she said curiously, 'How come you know its nickname. . .urban street tiger?'

'I *do* know something about bikes,' he said casually. 'I used to have a Triumph Bonneville.'

Chloe's eyes popped.

'You did?'

'Hmm. Just because I drive an old Rover now, and am bogged down with family responsibilities, it doesn't mean I've got one foot in the grave, you know. I got rid of the bike because I never seemed to get the chance to ride it.'

His voice became brisk and impersonal again as he went on to say, 'When you've had a coffee—and made me one—we'll discuss yesterday's fiasco.'

'It was no fiasco on my part!' she flung at him from the doorway.

'I don't recall saying it was.'

She wasn't having that.

'You might not have said it in so many words, but you didn't have to. When you phoned last night your manner was enough.'

'Chloe! I'd had a long and tiring day, and had popped into the pub for half an hour to unwind, only to find someone under our jurisdiction breaking the regulations regarding rabies. It was enough to make anyone tetchy. I'm sorry, and, having said that, let's be seeing the culprit's signature. Without it, we're in lumber.'

She opened her bag and handed over the notice that she'd got the Greek captain to sign. Saracen's keen eyes went over it and he nodded. 'That's OK, then. *We* can relax, which is more than that silly fool will be able to do. He could be fined anything between four hundred and two thousand pounds when it goes to court.'

'Why *do* they take animals on board?' she asked soberly.

'I don't know,' he replied, 'unless it's because they can't bear to be separated from them, or haven't got anyone to leave them with while they're away. . .no fixed abode, maybe.'

When she took the coffee in he was studying the World Health report from Geneva on infected areas where shipping might have to dock, and he said, 'A grim cocktail this lot appears to be—cholera, typhus, Lassa fever, poliomyelitis. . .and, yes. . .the plague. The rats bring that with them. Let's hope there aren't any infected rodents heading in this direction. We don't often find infestations on ships these days.'

'Did you have any success with your house sale?' she asked, on the point of going back into the kitchen.

'Yes, I think so. Completion should take place at eleven-thirty today with a bit of luck.'

'So you managed to coerce them?'

His head came up at that. 'I'm not exactly the Gestapo, Chloe. I persuaded them. . .yes. It turned out to be a minor problem regarding the roof of the conservatory that the two solicitors had blown up out of all proportion.'

'Good,' she said sweetly. 'So that's two problems solved. Your house sale. . .and the signature you so much wanted to see.'

He glanced at her sharply but let the sarcasm pass, and instead asked, 'So Friday night is on, is it?'

'Yes. The concert starts at half-past seven. It's only a short distance from where I live. So if you bring Lucy into Manchester I'll meet you outside. Will you stay in the area, or go back to Eastham and then drive back again?'

'I don't know. I'll decide that on the night,' was his

reply, and Chloe wondered what he would find to do to occupy himself if he decided to stay.

'I suppose Saturday would have been a better day for you,' she said, 'as you wouldn't have been working all day, but I've got an engagement on Saturday night.'

She'd promised to go out with Mike, and as it was their first date she wasn't going to start altering the arrangement. . .and the pop concert on Friday *was* the best thing for someone like Lucy.

'Friday suits me fine,' he told her. '*I* also have an engagement on Saturday. . .in Manchester. I'm taking someone to the theatre, and I wouldn't want to be chauffeuring Lucy around at the same time.'

Something in his tone told her that it was a woman. Men didn't speak about their own sex like that, and she wondered why she didn't feel pleased for him. The man couldn't be expected to live like a monk. He might be the king pin as far as Port Health was concerned, but his domestic set-up didn't sound too happy with a daughter at a difficult age and a frail mother holding the reins when he was absent. She wouldn't have thought he'd had time to get to know anybody at this end yet, but she'd already decided that most women would come running when a man as attractive as Thomas Saracen crooked his finger, and as she tried to bring Mike's cheerful face to mind Chloe hoped that her boss's theatre companion would know how to stand to attention, or bow the knee!

On the Friday morning Tom said, 'The *Celtic Lad* had been docked on the Weaver for the past three days, filling up with calcium chloride. She's leaving at ten o'clock today to catch the tide at Eastham, and I thought that as neither of us are familiar with the river, and as it comes under Port Health jurisdiction, we might sail with her through the various locks.

Chloe had just arrived. Her hair lay flat against her head from the weight of her helmet, and her cheeks were glowing from the fresh spring morning she'd just driven through. Saracen was looking her over with his keen blue gaze, and she would have dearly liked to know what he saw, but he was waiting for a reply to his suggestion, and if she didn't get a move-on he would be tapping his foot!

'I'd like that,' she told him. 'I'd like it a lot. The famous Anderton Lift is only a couple of hundred yards from where the *Celtic Lad* is berthed, if I'm not mistaken. It would be interesting to see it.'

She paused. Now was the moment for him to start airing his knowledge, but surprisingly he didn't. He just said quietly, 'So put me in the picture.'

Chloe gave a short amazed laugh. He actually didn't know!

'It was used at one time to lift barges that came along the Weaver, to the height of the Trent Canal thirty feet above, and vice versa, but now it lies idle, has done for some years. James Hanbury told me that funds had been made available for its repair, but he didn't think the amount on offer was enough.'

'That's a sight I would like to have seen. . .a barge being lifted that height,' he said.

'Me too,' she enthused, 'but sadly that's not possible these days.'

'Nevertheless, it will be worth a look,' Tom Saracen said. 'I'll give you ten minutes and then we're off.'

'Your vehicle, or mine?' she asked jokingly.

'Why? Have you got a spare helmet?'

Chloe eyed him warily. He didn't mean it, did he?

'I think there's one in the cupboard,' she said weakly. 'It was left on the dockside and brought in here until it was claimed. It isn't exactly trendy, though.'

'I suppose you mean it won't match up with the urban street tiger. Well, I'm not bothered if you aren't. It's too nice a morning to be closeted in the car.'

She would rather be closeted in the car, she thought, than have his body pressed up against hers on the bike, his hard chest brushing against her back, his knees slotted behind hers, and his breath on her neck. She wouldn't be able to steer straight.

Seemingly unaware of her reluctance, he was rummaging in the cupboard, and when he held an old-fashioned white helmet aloft Chloe knew she had fallen into a pit of her own making.

It was exactly as she'd feared. She was so conscious of him seated behind her that her hold on the hand grips was like jelly, and after a couple of false starts he murmured in her ear, 'Not much of a tigress today, are we?'

'More like a lamb to the slaughter,' she murmured.

His voice was there again. 'Just drive it, eh, Chloe, and stop acting like a nervous virgin?'

'I *am* a virgin,' she snapped back unthinkingly.

She couldn't see his face, but there was mockery in his voice as he said, 'I don't recollect asking for confirmation of that, but I *have* noted it.'

At that she put her foot down with such force that he almost fell off the back, and, blanking his disturbing nearness firmly out of her mind, she pointed the bike towards Northwich, and zoomed off.

'Port Health,' Tom Saracen informed a grey-haired man in a dark blue suit who was standing beside the *Celtic Lad*, measuring the depth of the water with a plumb line.

'The captain's on board,' the man called over his shoulder, and they proceeded up a small wooden ramp on to the deck.

The officer in question looked up in surprise when they appeared in the doorway of his cabin.

'Port Health?' he questioned. 'What's brought *you* on board? We're not due for an inspection for another four months.'

'Nothing of that nature,' Tom said. 'We'd like to sail down to the Ship Canal with you, if that's convenient. I'm Tom Saracen, chief port health officer, and this is my assistant, Chloe Cavendish. We're both new to the area and it would give us a chance to view the Weaver.'

'Sure,' the captain said easily. 'Welcome aboard.'

'Thanks,' Tom told him, 'but first we want to take a quick look at the Anderton Lift. You're not leaving immediately, are you?'

'In fifteen minutes,' the captain answered. 'As long as you're back by then.'

As they walked beside the tranquil river, past where Chloe had left the bike, Tom Saracen suddenly gripped her arm and brought her to a halt.

'Look there,' he said softly, and coming swiftly towards them was a wild mink, its beautiful black coat gleaming in the morning sun. As they watched, motionless, it streaked behind one of the wheels of the bike, and to their amazement came out with a tiny replica of itself clutched in its mouth. It disappeared into the bushes and then came back again, and repeated the exercise twice more, so that in all three tiny absconders had been returned to the safety of the nest.

Chloe's eyes misted. The mother instinct was strong in animals, but she and the man at her side had both found that it wasn't always so with humans.

'How lovely,' she breathed. 'She was prepared to risk our presence to get her little ones back to safety.'

'I agree,' he said sombrely, as if his thoughts had been running on the same lines as her own. 'The trouble is that since the activists released them from the mink farms they're running wild all over the countryside, and multiplying rapidly.'

His grip was still on her sleeve and as Chloe looked down on his capable fingers she wondered how it would feel to have his touch on her skin. Uncomfortable at her imaginings, she jerked out of his grasp and moved forward abruptly, only to go sprawling over a tree root, but before she hit the ground he caught her in his arms, and as he held her close she wasn't surprised to find that she liked it, just the same as she'd known deep down that his presence behind her on the bike was exciting.

However, the pleasurable moment was soon at an end. His face was closing up and he was putting her away from him, and she was reminded that here was a man who didn't think too kindly of her own sex, because a woman who'd loved the sea more than her child had hurt him more than he cared to admit.

But *she* wasn't like that, she thought rebelliously. The barren years with just her mother's brittle company had made her vow that when she found a man to love he and the fruit of their marriage would come before all else. They would have what Tom Saracen had been denied, and what her mother had never given her father and herself.

CHAPTER FOUR

THE Anderton Lift rose gauntly out of the still basin that was the turning point for vessels using the Weaver. It had the desolate look of mechanical equipment no longer in use, and as Chloe observed its blackened structure rising sturdily upwards to where the neat Trent Mersey Canal flowed, she could imagine a brightly coloured barge being drawn upwards, or lowered, from one waterway to another in its strong embrace.

'Sad to see a thing like that lying dormant,' Tom Saracen said, 'but a lot of worthwhile things are cast aside to make way for progress, if it can be called that.'

A blast on the ship's hooter indicating that departure time had arrived prevented further conversation, and they made their way back to the *Celtic Lad*.

As it moved smoothly away from the quayside Chloe saw that the man who had been measuring the depth of the water was at the wheel, and he introduced himself as the river pilot.

'I take her as far as March Locks,' he explained, 'and from then on it's the Ship Canal.'

He sounded friendly and competent and she took an instant liking to him.

'I have to watch the depth all the time as it soon sludges up,' he told her as he surveyed the water in front of them with bright grey eyes.

She nodded, entranced by the calm beauty of the scene around them. They had just left the chemical works behind, and there were huge oil tanks not far away, but the river, and the land bordering it, were examples of the English countryside at its best. A downy white swan passed by, and a blue heron eyed them haughtily from among swaying reeds. Chloe smiled. This was a far cry from rabies, rats and toxic substances, and yet they were just as responsibile for the health of the river and its navigators as they were for those who sailed the great canal.

As she let out a sigh of pleasure Chloe found Tom Saracen beside her, and when he commented, 'It's hard to believe that the Ship Canal with all its trappings of shipping and industry is only a stone's throw away, isn't it?' she smiled up at him.

They'd been thinking the same thing. . .a harmony of separate minds, and as they stood together on the bridge she was acutely aware of him once more, of his nearness, his masculinity, and the fact that she was far too interested in this widower who had a jaundiced view of women.

'That's Saltersford Locks ahead,' the pilot said, breaking into her thoughts. 'We'll be there in about fifteen minutes if you've any Port Health duties to carry out.'

'We'll take a sample of drinking water while we're there,' Tom said. 'It's important that we keep an eye on the purity of all water that's pumped on to ships for drinking purposes. I've just checked with the captain that there's no problem with their supply.'

There was a scattering of cottages on the lockside, and a huge sluice gate behind them that was used to prevent the nearby town being flooded when the river was high. As they went ashore Chloe took a special container out of her bag, and, leaving Tom Saracen with the lockmaster, she took a sample of water from the draw-off point at the hydrant and, after labelling it carefully, returned it to her bag, until such time as they returned to the office, from where it would be sent to the public health analyst. There had been no reports of problems with drinking water on any vessel in recent days, but Port Health took no chances, and supplies were checked every three months at the minimum.

They left the *Celtic Lad* at Eastham Locks, and once they were on dry land again Tom Saracen said, 'Now we've got the problem of getting you back to where you left the bike, and as my car is still at Port House it's going to be a bit tricky. Let's have a word with Port Control to see if anyone is going in our direction.'

They were in luck. One of the men was finishing early, and as he lived in the Runcorn area he volunteered to drop Chloe off where she'd left the bike, and then deposit her companion back at Port House.

Once in the car the two men chatted amicably about various things, and Chloe, seated in the back, was only too happy to remain silent. The trip down the river with the man seated in front of her had been delightful. They had gone for almost a day without any criticism on his part, or taking umbrage on her own. Remembering those few brief seconds when he'd held her close, Chloe had a strange feeling that *they* would be part of the idyll she would remember the most.

Her thoughts switched to the night ahead. She was taking his daughter to hear Take That, and although she was only too happy to do so, not having forgotten how miserable and uppity a thirteen-year-old could feel, she couldn't help wishing that she hadn't been so adamant that three was a crowd.

Tom came to stand by her as she unlocked the bike, and told her, 'Go straight home. If anything has come up at the office I'll deal with it, and we'll see you at. . . what time?'

'Seven o'clock outside the theatre. I managed to get tickets, so there's no need for us to queue.'

'Right. We'll be there. . .and. . .thanks again, Chloe.'

She smiled. 'I only hope that Lucy is into Take That.'

'You're kidding! Of course she is!'

His eyes were less guarded than usual, his mouth soft, and as Chloe watched the pale spring sun throw the contours of his face into shadow it was clear to her that when it came to his daughter Saracen's hard core disappeared. Hadn't he given up a job that he must have loved, and changed careers, to be with her, and so whatever he was on the outside—defensive, cool, withdrawn—inside there had to be a heart, and a big one at that?

But what was the matter with her? she asked herself as she drove home. Tom Saracen wouldn't care a damn what the likes of Chloe thought about him. He was a mature man. . .who knew where he was going, and if he *had* decided that he wasn't going to travel alone, it certainly wouldn't be with a young graduate like herself.

'You must be crazy,' she said out loud. 'You haven't

known the man five minutes and here you are soliloquizing over him like some teenybopper!'

In spite of her self-chastisement, it didn't stop her from eyeing the clothes in her wardrobe with a thoughtful eye. Tonight would be the first time that the mesmeric Thomas had seen her out of uniform and, though it might be only briefly, she couldn't resist the urge to make an impact. If she'd been going anywhere else but to a crowded pop concert she would have chosen a glamorous full-skirted dress that would show off her firm breasts and slender waist, but not this time. She was going to dress down rather than up, for Lucy's sake, and so after showering, and brushing her gold bob until it shone, she dressed in a long white shirt and black leggings, replacing the milky pearl studs she would normally have worn in her ears with a pair of gold hoops.

When her mother came strolling in after a late-afternoon bridge session she eyed Chloe distastefully and enquired where she was off to.

'I'm taking my boss's young daughter to a pop concert,' Chloe told her, ignoring the critical stare.

'Really? Have you got your ear plugs?' Lorraine wanted to know.

'I don't need them,' Chloe told her with a smile. 'I'll enjoy it just as much as she will.'

'Yes, well, I'll be out when you get back,' her mother said. 'I'm dining at the Murchisons' and they never eat until late. The chauffeur will bring me back.'

They were there before her, the striking dark-haired man and the young girl so like him, standing apart from the jostling youthful crowd pouring into the theatre foyer. Lucy's cheeks were pink with excitement, but as she approached Chloe saw apprehension in the girl's dark eyes and she thought it was no wonder. The child was about to spend the evening with someone that she'd met only once, and that for a few fleeting seconds. Unease stirred inside her. It would have been more sensible to have waited until she knew Lucy better before making the rash offer, but how would she have accomplished that? Her father was hardly likely to be urging his assistant to call round for a game of Scrabble!

There didn't seem to be any doubts on his part, however. When he saw her the creases across his brow disappeared, and he nodded in brief greeting as he propelled Lucy towards her with his arm around her shoulders.

'Hello, Lucy,' she said with a reassuring smile. 'Nice to meet you again.'

The girl responded with a shy smile of her own, but didn't speak. Her silence was compensated for by the difference in her attitude from the last time. There was no sulkiness tonight, and Chloe began to feel more relaxed. Maybe she *had* hit the jackpot with her suggestion, and Lucy had forgotten for a little while that she'd come to live in a strange place.

If she'd expected any bouquets with regard to her appearance from Tom Saracen, he wasn't handing any out. He'd given her a long keen look when they came face to face, but he hadn't exactly stepped back in amazement to proclaim the beauty of the butterfly that had emerged from its Port Health chrysalis, but then he wouldn't, would he?

For one thing she wasn't dressed to please *him*, and

for another flattery wasn't his style. On top of that, although her skin was smooth and creamy, her teeth even, her nose small and straight, and her eyes light brown with golden flecks, the combination didn't make it a face to turn heads. It was an open, honest face, averagely attractive, and she thought that any man who was looking for more would have to seek elsewhere.

If she had a feature that did set her apart it was her hair. Straight and shining in its attractive short cut, it framed her face, and tonight, next to the dark locks of Saracen and his daughter, its sheen was even more pronounced.

He was frowning again as he said, 'I'm going to have to dash, I'm afraid. I'd intended browsing around Manchester but it's not to be. A call came through on the car phone as we were driving here. There's a health problem on one of the ships that docked earlier in the day. . .a sick woman, of all things. I presume she must have only just become ill as there was no word about it earlier. Martin Page, the MO, is out for the evening, and they're trying to locate him so that we can meet up there.'

His frown was deepening. 'The trouble is that I may not be back in time for the end of the concert. If I'm not, will you take Lucy to your place, and I'll pick her up there? If I do make it in time I'll be waiting in the side-street there. OK?'

'Yes, of course,' she said immediately.

He was ready for off, the job tugging at him, and she said, 'What a drag, your having to go all the way back.'

He smiled for the first time and gave Lucy a quick

squeeze. 'It's the lesser of two evils. It could have been *your* turn to be on call, which would have meant *me* having to sit through Take That.'

Lucy didn't stamp, shout, or scream during the concert. She sat quite still in her baggy sweater, long skirt, and clumsy shoes, with an ecstatic smile on her face, and Chloe hid a smile of her own. It appeared that it *had* been a good idea, after all. As she looked at Saracen's teenage daughter she was satisfied that whatever moping she'd been doing of late, tonight didn't come into it. She was completely happy.

They'd chatted while they were waiting for the concert to start. At least, Chloe had; Lucy's contribution to the conversation had been mostly shy monosyllables as she had gently probed into Lucy's feelings about the move. Lucy *had* vouchsafed one piece of information, though, and it had been illuminating with regard to her having had second thoughts about coming up north.

'When Dad asked me if I'd mind living in a different place I said it was all right by me,' she'd explained awkwardly. 'I'd just fallen out with my best friend, Sophie, and I didn't care where we went to live. The quarrel lasted for ages, but on our last night at the old house she came and made it up.'

Good for you, Sophie, Chloe thought wryly. Who better than one teenage girl to put the mockers on it for another? 'So you didn't want to go then?'

'No.'

'Does your dad know why you've been miserable?'

'No.'

'Don't you think he should?'

'Yes.'

'It would make it easier for him to undertand what's
been bugging you. You owe him that, Lucy.'

'Yes, I know,' she'd agreed uncomfortably.

'He loves you a lot, doesn't he?' she'd questioned
gently.

'Yes, I suppose he does.'

'Well, then, why not let him see that you're not a
little girl any more, that you can cope? If you make
the best of it, I can guarantee that once you start
school you'll soon feel as if you belong. It's Easter
next week, so you haven't long to wait, and if you
enjoy tonight there's no reason why we can't do it
again, is there?'

Lucy's eyes had lit up.

'With Dad?'

'Er—yes. . .if he wants to come, I suppose, but you
heard what he said when he was going.'

His daughter had smiled. 'He was only teasing. . .
just letting us know that it's not his kind of music.'

At that moment the lights had dimmed and her
young companion's eyes had become riveted on the
stage for the rest of the evening.

When it was over and the applause had died down
they made their way towards the street where Tom
had said he would be parked, and to Chloe's surprise
the car was there. As they drew near she saw that he
was asleep behind the wheel, still in his Port Health
clothes that he hadn't had time to change in the rush
to get Lucy to Manchester.

As they observed him through the window Lucy said
softly, 'Good old Dad. He does everything for Gran
and me.' Then casually, as if it was of no moment, 'Do
you know that my mum is dead?'

'Yes, he told me,' Chloe said carefully.

'He did!' she exclaimed. 'That's strange. He doesn't usually talk about her.'

'It just came up in conversation, that's all,' Chloe explained, trying to sound casual.

She needn't have worried. Lucy was on to another train of thought. 'My gran says will you come to dinner one night next week, as a thank-you for taking me out?'

Chloe eyed the sleeping man in the car and didn't know what to say. From what she'd seen of him so far she would expect that he wasn't the type to mix business with pleasure. . .and all things being right the invitation should come from him. But if she waited for that, it might never come! Unable to subdue her desire to see more of him in the family mould, she said, 'Tell your gran thanks. I'd like that, but do please make sure that it's all right with your dad.'

Lucy stared at her.

'Of course it will be. You work with him, don't you?'

'Yes, I do, and that's exactly what I mean. . .and now, sadly, we're going to have to disturb him.'

He looked younger and, of all things, defenceless in sleep. There was dark stubble on his jaw, and a lock of the thick black hair had fallen on to his brow. His hands were slack beside him on the seat, and she wanted to take one of them in hers, and gently bring him back to wakefulness, but not so Lucy. She was sliding into the seat beside him and shaking his shoulder.

When his eyes opened it was Chloe that they focused on, watching him through the car window. Winding it down, he said drowsily, 'You look different, and where's your hard hat?'

She laughed. 'You've already seen me once tonight, or maybe you didn't. . .and I'm off duty.'

He stretched wearily. 'More than I can say.'

'What was the problem?'

'Nothing that I'm going to bother you with at this time of night. We'll discuss it on Monday.' As he switched on the engine he added, 'Are you getting in? Or are you intending standing there all night? Only I'm not leaving you here in the middle of Manchester's nightlife.'

'I'm used to it,' she told him airily. 'This is where I live, don't forget.'

'I don't care a damn where you live. Just get in!' he growled. 'I want to know that you're home safely.'

When they stopped outside the huge apartment complex Lucy's eyes goggled, and when Chloe invited them in for a coffee she was halfway out of the car before he'd had the chance to reply, but he pulled her back.

'No, but thanks just the same,' he said. 'It's late and my mother is alone.' As she got out of the car he leaned out of the window and brought her back to earth with a bump. 'Have a nice evening tomorrow.'

'You too,' she said weakly.

'I shall try,' he said soberly, and as she went into the elegant entrance hall of the apartments it came into her mind that he wasn't exactly bursting with enthusiasm. . .but then neither was she, and it wasn't fair to Mike. It wasn't his fault that she seemed to have picked up a virus, a new strain that was called Thomas Saracen.

* * *

Contrary to expectations, Chloe enjoyed the evening with Mike. He took her to a new Italian restaurant, and there was lots of laughing and amiable discussion. When he left her outside the apartment block he kissed her meaningfully, and though she responded it was with less enthusiasm than his, for although she'd enjoyed his company she knew that Mike would never make her blood warm or her heart beat faster.

They were of a similar age, which was supposed to be a good thing in a relationship, but the fact remained that she wasn't looking for somebody like Mike, and, that being so, what was she looking for?

Nothing. . .nobody. . .until a week ago. She'd been contented with her lot, the new job, the bike, her friends at the Honda club, and now she was dithering like a. . .nervous virgin? Hardly. She wasn't nervous, merely confused, though the virgin part was correct, as she'd so rashly admitted to the man who'd likened her as such, and, as she took off the blue silk blouse and smart white trousers that she'd worn for her date with Mike, Chloe eyed her slender nakedness in the mirror.

When they'd come across the mink beside the Weaver, Tom had gripped her sleeve, and when she'd stumbled he'd caught her and held her close for a second. In that moment she'd experienced a desire to feel his touch on her bare skin, and as she observed her firm breasts the nipples sprang to hardness, and there was a moistness between her untouched thighs that came from the ache inside her.

On Monday morning Chloe was hoping that when she saw Tom Saracen he might have less appeal for her, that after being almost constantly in his company over the past week she would find that her emotions had settled down. She'd been bowled over by his physical attractions, along with admiration, albeit reluctant, for the way he'd slotted himself into the job with such speed and efficiency, and now she was hoping that she might see him merely in the role of senior colleague.

It was a vain hope. Whatever had happened over the weekend had put him back on his stride. She'd felt compassion for the tired man of Friday night, but he was gone, and behind the desk was the keen-eyed martinet in a crisp white shirt and a Port Health tie that was emblazoned with a sea-dog, a mythical talbot-like beast by the name of Cerebos.

But wasn't that how she wanted him to be? Mr Efficiency Plus. . .her boss, yet in that moment she was aware that it made no difference what hat he had on. Tom Saracen was in her blood!

'Morning, Chloe,' he said with the crispness that went with his appearance, and before she had time to answer, 'Are you aware that the importation of goods made partly or completely of goat hair is forbidden under the prevention of anthrax regulations?'

Her eyes widened. 'Why? What's the problem? I haven't had anything to do with goat hair!'

He gave his dry laugh. 'Of course you haven't, but I was reminded of the fact yesterday.'

'I'm not with you. In what way?' she questioned.

'Because one of the dratted animals decimated the vegetable garden at the back of my house. If I could have got my hands on it there would have been an *exportation* order on *that* beast!'

Chloe laughed. 'What did Lucy have to say?'

'She laughed, like you are doing. By the way, I don't know what magic wand you waved on Friday night, but my daughter has been almost back to her old self these last two days.'

'I didn't wave any wand,' she said quietly. 'We had a chat which might have helped a bit. . .and she loved the concert. Has she told you about her friend Sophie?'

He sighed. 'Yes, she *has*, and I've told her that Sophie can visit us whenever she wants. I could have shaken her! First of all for saying that she was happy to move, when really it was because she'd fallen out with her friend, and secondly for not telling me when something was hurting. Now it's too late, we're here, and if she's sorry, *I'm* not. I like the northern people; I find them hospitable and down to earth.'

It was generous praise, not exactly what she'd have liked him to say, but what did she expect? It was most unlikely that he would start eulogising about herself, or any other woman for that matter. As far as Tom Saracen was concerned they were the *unfair* sex.

'What was the problem on Friday night?' she asked, thinking that Lucy's youthful aberrations had received enough criticism.

'Possibly malaria,' he said briefly. 'The English captain had his wife on board, and, whereas he and the crew make frequent trips to the Ivory Coast, it was the lady's first time, and she must have been bitten by a mosquito.

'She'd suddenly started to be ill, showing all the signs of malaria—shivering, fever, headache and vomiting—and it's about right for the incubation period. . . twelve days since the ship left Africa. She could have been bitten any time while they were there. Although, having said that, we both know that the malaria bug can lie dormant for a long time if she's been on antimalarial drugs, but I doubt that. It was a spur of the moment thing, his taking her along.

'The worst kind of malaria is the falciparum strain which attacks *all* the red blood cells, whereas the other types destroy only young or old cells, and I'm afraid it's the one that is usually picked up in Africa. The others are more likely to come from the Indian subcontinent.

'Needless to say, Martin Page had her admitted to hospital, as she'll need blood tests every few hours to ascertain whether it *is* malaria. If it's not then we'll be anxious to know what it *is*, as we don't want our riparian boroughs being swamped with anything that's epidemical.'

'What drugs do they normally prescribe for it?' Chloe asked.

'Chloroquine, or, if it transpires that the disease is resistant to it, they often use common quinine to get rid of the parasites in the blood.'

'Aren't we told that the World Health Organization conducts a massive malaria control programme?' she questioned.

'Yes, and it's true, but progress is held back because mosquitoes have developed resistance to insecticides, and in many areas the parasites they leave behind have become immune to antimalaria drugs.'

'I see.'

He smiled his dry smile.

'Yes, I believe you do.'

'How would you have felt if you'd gone on board

and found the sick woman to be the captain?' she asked impulsively, and was immediately put in her place.

'Exactly the same as I would have felt about any sick person,' he said coldly. 'I've no objection to women at sea. . .or in Port Health, if you've any doubts on that score. What I *do* object to, though, is having assumptions made with regard to my opinions and behaviour.'

'You *did* refer to us as the unfair sex,' she protested, her face flaming as she wished that she'd kept her mouth shut.

'It would seem that your memory is at fault as well as your judgement,' he said in the same icy tone. 'I remember referring to the *fair* sex in your presence, and though I might have cast some doubt on the truth of the words, I don't recall rephrasing them.'

She swallowed hard. It was getting out of hand. She'd made a thoughtless remark and was paying for it. What had possessed her? Was it the desire to get him to talk about his dead wife. . .a ghoulish sort of curiosity? Or was it envy because the woman had been married to Tom Saracen, and there was a yearning inside *her* to take his wife's place?

Chloe brought her thoughts under control with an effort. There was something else she had to say, and there would be nothing tactless about it this time. It would come straight from the heart.

'I'm so sorry,' she said with desperate earnestness. 'Do please forgive me. It was a stupid thing to say.'

He didn't say he would. He didn't say he wouldn't. He just eyed her thoughtfully and said, 'Bickering wasn't on today's agenda, but lots of other things are.

I want to leave my desk clear tonight as I'm at the Port of London tomorrow for the Imported Foods Committee meeting, among others. You'll be in charge.'

He didn't comment further, but if he'd added 'So just watch it!' she wouldn't have been surprised.

When it was time to pack up for the day Chloe said awkwardly, 'Your mother invited me to dinner one night this week, but as you're in London tomorrow, and it's Easter on Friday, perhaps it would be better if. . .I. . .er. . .'

The blue eyes were boring into hers.

'Are you saying you don't want to come?'

'No! Of course not,' she stammered. 'I just thought that after this morning you mightn't. . .'

'Thursday all right?' he asked, breaking into her mumblings.

'Er. . .yes. . .if it's all right with you.'

'Do me a favour, Chloe!' he said with an exasperated snort. 'Would I be seconding the invitation if it wasn't?'

'No, I suppose not,' she admitted weakly, and, gathering her belongings together, went in search of the bike.

CHAPTER FIVE

'YOU'RE in charge,' Tom Saracen had said, which was fair comment as there were only two of them employed in the environmental health side of the port, but even so Chloe found that the charge lay heavy on her shoulders as she drove to work the following morning.

But the reality of it was that there *would* be times when she would have to cope alone, apart from Maureen's administrative assistance, and the sooner she accepted the fact, the better, she told herself.

Up to now she hadn't put a foot wrong, for the episode with the Greek captain and his dog had been no fault of hers, as Tom Saracen had been obliged to admit, and today. . . God willing. . .she intended to be as hiccup-free as all the other days since she'd started with Port Health.

A Panamanian vessel on its way to Canvey Island with a cargo of steel was on the list of ships to dock on the first tide of the day, and when Chloe realised that it was the first time it had been in the Port of Manchester she went on board to do an inspection.

When she'd appeared on deck some of the crew were there, and she was aware of dark eyes in swarthy faces lasciviously observing her trim coltish figure in the crisp white shirt and dark skirt, and eyeing the pale basque of her hair beneath the blue hard hat, their fascination no doubt born of the lack of fair-haired women in their native land.

It wasn't so with the captain. Like the rest of the crew he was Korean, but he was meticulously polite and respectful. The Maritime Declaration of Health that he presented to her showed that there were no health problems on his ship, and though the vessel was old Chloe wasn't surprised to find that he had an up-to-date de-ratting certificate that had been issued in Malaysia.

James Hanbury, Tom and Maureen had all surprised her by stating that in this day and age it was rare to find rats on a ship, but that the precautions taken against such an occurrence were never relaxed.

The ship's galley was clean, the cabins in reasonable condition, and after taking a water sample from the kitchen and another from the shower head to check for legionella, Chloe left the HIV video with the captain, promising to return for it in the afternoon.

When she got back to the office Lucy was waiting, and Chloe greeted her with a mixture of surprise and pleasure, receiving a bouncy smile in return.

Maureen was there, too, and she told Chloe, 'Lucy and I have been getting acquainted. She tells me that she has no friends here, and I've suggested that she comes round to my house to meet the boys. She and my eldest will be in the same class when she starts school, so it's a good opportunity for them to get to know each other. The three of them could play tapes or go swimming, or whatever else they want to do, as long as it's all right with her dad.'

'I'll ask him when he gets back from London tonight,' Lucy promised enthusiastically.

'How's the house coming along?' Chloe asked when

Maureen had gone downstairs to use the computer. 'Have you got it straight yet?'

'Nearly,' she said. 'Although Gran has a bad leg she gets around. . .and *I've* been helping.'

'Good for you!' Chloe applauded, and then, 'Are you aware that I'm coming to dine with you on Thursday?'

'Yes. Dad told me. I told you it would be all right, didn't I?'

'Yes, you did,' Chloe agreed soberly, as the memory of the short acerbic exchange of words that had preceded the invitation came back to her.

It was then that he'd said he had nothing against women at sea. . .or in Port Health, but she wasn't convinced he'd meant it. She still felt it necessary to tread carefully with her senior officer, as one moment he would applaud her, and the next come down in criticism. Well, there would be no need for that today. She was keyed in to the job, and intended to hold the fort again like a seasoned campaigner.

With Lucy's visit, and various other matters to attend to, it was on her way home that Chloe called to pick up the HIV video on loan, and as she parked the bike beside the Panamanian ship the light was fading fast. There was no activity to be seen this time, no dark-skinned crew on the mast or on deck, just one light showing in a cabin down below.

For some reason that she couldn't explain she unfastened her crash helmet and took it off, and, swinging it from her hand, walked quickly up the ramp and on to the deserted deck. It looked as if they'd all gone ashore for the evening, except for maybe the captain, who'd stayed behind to hand back the video. That *had*

better be it, she thought. She was hungry, and ready
to go home, and it would all be wasted effort if there
was no one available to give her what she'd come for.

She went swiftly down a narrow flight of stairs
towards the lighted cabin and was reaching for the
door-handle when she was gripped from behind by a
pair of sinewy arms. The shock of it froze her in terror.
She'd been uneasy from the moment of arriving on the
quayside, and now she knew why. Somebody *had*
stayed behind, and she didn't think it was the polite
captain.

The man's hot breath was on her neck, his hands
already inside her clothes, and in desperation she
swung the helmet up with all her might and gave her
molester an almighty whack in the face. She couldn't
see him in the darkness, but his strength was obvious,
and it was surprise rather than pain that made him
slacken his grip. In that second Chloe twisted herself
free, opened the cabin door, and flung herself through
it, sliding the heavy bolt into place with frantic fingers.

There then followed an onslaught on the door,
banging and thumping to a degree that made her think
he was using his shoulder. She crouched trembling in
a corner of the room. He'd been thwarted and didn't
like it. *She* liked it even less, and the tears began to
run down her cheeks.

Where *was* everybody? It could be hours before the
captain and crew returned, and by that time her sex-
starved attacker would have broken down the solid
timbers of the door.

Suddenly there was silence; the battering had
ceased, and her fear lessened, but only for as long as
it took her to reason that he might be trying another

tack, enticing her out by making her think he'd given up and gone.

She sank down on the crumpled bunk. This wasn't the captain's cabin. It smelt stale and was cluttered with dirty clothes. There was a half-eaten meal on the table, and whoever it belonged to must be the man who had awaited her return, and pounced the moment she'd boarded.

Chloe gave a gulping sob. Tom had warned her about seamen, desperate for a woman after weeks at sea, and she'd accepted that there might be a small element of risk, but never this, and *she* was partly to blame. She'd boarded a deserted ship without assessing the consequences, and now she was in a terrifying situation. Tom would go crazy when he found out, and as for herself, the thought of losing her virginity to a lusting foreign seaman in a squalid cabin was a thought so horrendous that she began to retch.

The silence continued and Chloe waited. The desire to unbolt the door and run for it was overwhelming, but greater than that was the fear of those strangling arms around her, and so she resigned herself to sitting it out.

An hour went by, and then another, and, unable to stand the suspense any longer, she was reaching her hand out for the bolt when she heard footsteps on the deck above. As she stood frozen in mute terror, with her hand still outstretched, they began to come down the narrow stairway and stopped outside the door of the cabin.

Was it the man who'd attacked her, she thought frantically, come back for another onslaught on the door? Or some of the crew? Or was it someone else?

It *was* someone else, and as he bellowed her name she went weak with relief.

'Chloe! Are you in there?' Tom Saracen was demanding to know.

She tried to speak, but all that came out was a squeak, like that of a frightened kitten. Drawing back the bolt slowly, she opened the door a couple of inches, so traumatised that, although she knew it was his voice, she couldn't believe that it was really him. Then he was thrusting it open, and she fell sobbing into his arms. . .the right ones, she thought gratefully, not those of a swarthy lusting stranger.

'What the hell is going on?' he asked roughly, his chin resting above her golden crown as she clung to him.

'I came back to collect the video,' she gulped, 'and there was no one here, just a light on in one of the cabins. I thought it would be the captain waiting for me, but it wasn't. One of the crew must have stayed behind and he pounced on me.' She shuddered against the hardness of his chest and he cradled her more closely. 'I managed to get away and locked myself in the cabin. I've been in there for hours.'

Lifting a strand of her hair, he let it slide through his fingers, growling as he did so, 'You should have kept *this* covered up. If you go flaunting your Saxon fairness among these seamen it's all you can expect.'

Chloe stiffened in his arms. When she'd opened the door he had been the most beautiful sight in the world. She hadn't questioned how or why he was there, just basked in the exquisite relief of his presence, but now he was putting the blame on *her* again, making it look as if it was her own fault that she'd almost been raped. Her eyes bright with outrage, she threw off his hold and faced him.

'Thanks a bunch!' she cried. 'So it's all right with you if some sex-starved sailor decides to molest me!'

'Now you're being stupid,' he said patiently, as if he hadn't already accused her of that. 'Why do you think I came haring on to the ship when I saw your bike on the quay? Certainly not because I was prepared to let you fight your own battles!' His voice roughened with an emotion she couldn't identify. 'But Chloe, supposing I hadn't seen the bike. . .supposing he'd come back. . .it's obvious that he's done a runner for the time being, but what would have you done then?'

She had a grip on herself now and said flippantly, 'Jumped overboard, or hit him again with my helmet, which is the reason why I'm flaunting my hair, as you describe it. When I came aboard earlier I was wearing my hard hat. This time I was on my way home.'

As he opened his mouth to condem her attitude they heard voices on the quayside, and when they looked down some of the crew were approaching, their noisy laughter and singing indicating that they had been in one of the waterfront pubs.

When they saw the two Port Health officers looking down on them from the deck there was mild consternation, and Chloe saw one of them lower his head and move to the back of the group. The captain was among them and Tom told him grimly, 'One of your crew attacked my assistant earlier this evening, and if it hadn't been for her presence of mind it could have been a very serious incident. Which man was left on the ship when you went on shore?'

The slanting oriental eyes surveyed them blandly and he shrugged narrow shoulders. 'I not know. They have been on and off all the time.'

'Whose cabin is this?' Tom asked, pointing to the lighted room below.

'The mate's.'

'Where is he now?'

The captain turned and pointed to the man skulking at the back.

'Is that the man?' Tom asked of her.

'I don't know,' she whispered. 'I didn't see his face.'

'Then in that case there isn't much we can do,' he told her in a low voice. To the captain he said, 'I shall report this to the port authority, and if they decide to pass the matter on to the police your ship will be in trouble, Captain.'

The man gave an odd little bow as if accepting the castigation, and then led his crew back on board, with Tom Saracen and herself standing grimly to one side.

'Would you please get the video?' he requested coldly, and once the captain had produced it from out of his cabin Tom took her arm and said tersely, 'Let's go.' They returned to the quayside, leaving an uneasy silence behind them.

'I take it that you've inspected the ship?' he asked as Chloe breathed a sigh of relief at being back on shore.

She nodded.

'And?'

'No problems. . .until tonight.'

'So there's no need for another visit, and if there was *you* wouldn't be making it. I'm afraid that my threats were without substance. As there hasn't been an actual assault, and you can't identify your assailant, there is little we can do.'

She was about to unlock the bike, but he stopped her and said, 'Leave it here. It'll be safe enough. I'm going to take you home in my car. You're too shaken up to drive.'

His remarks about her hair still rankling, Chloe said flatly, 'There's no need. I can look after myself.'

His dark brows drew together.

'Oh, yes? Well, if tonight's an example, I think we'll have to agree to differ.'

He was opening the door of his car, and he said in the tone one would use to a wayward child, 'Get in, Chloe, and tell me what you've been doing today, apart from the nasty episode earlier.'

She began to shudder again. The memory of those horrifying moments on the darkened ship would be with her forever, but she wasn't going to admit it to doubting Thomas. He'd already made it clear that she'd behaved stupidly, and the annoying thing was that he was right. . .as always.

'I inspected the ship that we've just left,' she said, trying to keep her voice steady. 'Then I went on to Runcorn dock to supervise the unloading of a dry bulk cargo that the wind was blowing towards the town. When I pointed out the risk of dust pollution, the men dealing with its transfer to lorries stopped work until it was calmer, and accepted that the vehicles taking it along the motorway must be covered. In the early afternoon Lucy came into the office and I spent some time with her.'

'Lucy! Came into the office!' he exclaimed. 'Why did she do that?'

'I don't know, unless it was because she wanted a chat. Maybe she was at a loose end. She met Maureen while she was there, and our delightful administrator invited her to meet her two sons, subject to your approval. It would appear that one of them will be in Lucy's class when she starts school, so she will have one acquaintance at least.'

'I see,' he said thoughtfully, and she wondered if he would have been happier if Maureen's offspring had been girls.

Her voice hardened. 'And then. . .I called to pick up the HIV video on my way home. . .and you know the rest.'

'Yes, I most certainly do,' he agreed grimly. 'When I stumbled across your bike on the quayside, and you were nowhere to been seen, alarm bells rang immediately. I'd called at the office to drop off the paperwork I'd picked up in London, and as I was driving along the top road I saw what I thought was the outline of a bike on the quayside. When I drove down here to investigate, what did I find but the Fireblade.'

Chloe turned away, hunching her shoulder against the reprimand in his voice. The last thing she needed at this moment was to be in the company of a censorious perfectionist, and she cursed herself for letting him take charge when she could have been halfway home by now.

It seemed that he was tuned in to her thoughts. 'What's the matter? I suppose you're thinking how much quicker it would have been on the bike, eh? Well, if you are, it's just too bad. I don't want you involved in any more dangerous situations tonight, or

at any other time, for that matter, and that's why I'm
delivering you to your parent personally.'

She eyed him balefully. If he didn't stop treating her
like a child she would explode!

'You might be one of the world's achievers,' she
snapped, 'but even *you* can't manage that!'

'What?'

'To pass me over to my mother. She's never there
when I get in. To use a depressing though topical
phrase, we're ships that pass in the night, the only
difference being that she's a luxury liner, and I'm a
tug.'

'So you'll be alone?'

'Yes.'

'All night?'

'Most of it, I should imagine.'

They were almost at a branch road on the motorway,
and when they reached it he turned off, and within
seconds they were going back the way they had come.
She looked at him in amazement.

'Why did you do that?' she cried.

'There's no need to panic,' he said evenly. 'I promised to take you home and I *am*. The only difference
is we're going to *my* home, instead of yours. You
won't want to be on your own in that flat after what
has happened.'

He was right as usual. The thought of it didn't
appeal at all, but she wasn't going to admit it. She
wasn't going to refuse the chance to spend the night
with people she could trust, though what the elderly
Mrs Saracen would think of her son bringing home an
unexpected overnight visitor at this hour, she
didn't know.

'I've brought someone to stay, Mother,' Tom said as he ushered Chloe into a pleasant sitting-room where a coal fire was burning brightly.

His mother was seated in a high-backed chair with the calipered leg stretched out in front of her, and as she made to rise Chloe put out her hand.

'Please don't get up, Mrs Saracen,' she said quickly, her own trauma and exhaustion suddenly seeming less important beside an elderly lady with a bad leg who was having an unexpected lodger dumped on her without notice. Empty flat or not, she found herself wishing that she'd gone straight home.

'Absolutely,' he was agreeing in his usual brisk manner. 'Stay right where you are, Mother. I'll see to Chloe. You remember you met her briefly the other day? Well, she's had a rather nasty experience, and as there isn't likely to be anyone there when she gets home, I've brought her here.'

'And rightly so,' his mother agreed immediately with the same decisiveness as her son. 'Apart from being only too pleased to help, it will be good for Lucy and me to see a fresh face,' she said matter-of-factly, as if receiving a distressed young woman into her home late in the evening was the norm.

'Sit down,' Tom commanded, and, white-faced and weary, Chloe obeyed. 'I'm going to make you a cup of hot sweet tea, or maybe a stiff brandy would be better?'

'Tea will be fine,' she said meekly.

'Right, and then we'll feed you. *I* had my meal on the train, and Mum and Lucy will have eaten ages ago, but *you* must be starving. I'm not much of a cook, but

I can do the basics, and if you'll settle for that we're in business.'

If she'd been in better form Chloe might have taken him up on the fact that there was something he didn't excel at, but not tonight. Tomorrow she might be more like herself, but not now. She was hungry and exhausted, and absolutely miserable that Tom had caught her out in a humiliating situation, yet she was humbly grateful, too, that he'd rescued her from that dreadful cabin and the awful possibilities that went with it.

She was eating an omelette with slices of crusty bread, in a kitchen that was as big as the sitting-room and immaculately tidy, when music that had been churning out above ceased, and seconds later Lucy appeared in the doorway.

'Chloe!' she exclaimed with a beam that was a welcome in itself. 'What are *you* doing here?'

'She was late getting away from the office,' Tom interrupted from behind her, 'and I suggested that instead of going all the way to Manchester she stay here for the night.'

Chloe's white face had coloured up. He wouldn't want anything as sordid as the night's events to get to his young daughter's ears, and she couldn't blame him for that, but it didn't make *her* feel any better, even though she had been spared the embarrassment of having her foolishness related to someone else.

'I don't ever discuss my staff with anyone else,' he'd told her when she'd accused him of doing just that with Martin Page and discovered to her mortification that she'd made a mistake. The fact that he'd covered up for her now was proof of that. He was protecting his staff. That was all she was. . .a member of his staff, and the sooner she got that idea into perspective, the better, for the sake of the job. . .and for the sake of her peace of mind.

'I've changed my bed and put out pyjamas and a robe,' he was saying. 'You'll find them a bit roomy, I'm afraid, but better too big than too small.'

'Where will *you* sleep?' she asked uncomfortably, aware that if he amazed her by saying 'Beside you', she wouldn't say no.

'In the study. I have a couch in there. I've used it before, so you don't need to fret. By the way, what do you like for breakfast?'

He was being extremely thoughtful and hospitable in a businesslike sort of way, and she knew she ought to be grateful. She was. . .but it didn't stop her from wondering what he was thinking behind his impersonal concern, or from feeling herself to be an encumbrance.

'Just tea and toast will be fine,' she said uncomfortably, and was saved any further ministrations on his part by Lucy saying,

'You remember me telling you this afternoon that Dad had bought me a new Take That tape? Would you like to hear it?'

She didn't appear to be aware that their guest was under some constraint, and Chloe smiled. 'Yes, of course.' She couldn't deny the child the pleasure of playing it for her, even though all she wanted to do was curl up, bury her head beneath the bedclothes, and try to blot out one of the worst nights of her life, but Tom was shaking his head.

'Not tonight, Luce. Chloe isn't on top form. Maybe in the morning, eh?'

Lucy eyed them both curiously, and then nodded. 'Yes, all right, in the morning, but will there be time?'

'I'll make time,' Chloe promised, and was rewarded with a smile.

'Good. In that case, I'm going to make hot chocolate for Gran and me, and then I'm going to bed.'

She reached up to kiss her father's lean cheek and he ruffled her hair with a tender hand. Watching them, Chloe felt her heart twist. There were three generations in this house and they lived in harmony because they loved each other. Tom Saracen had no wife to love him, Lucy had no mother, but they had the woman who was watching them fondly from the kitchen doorway to bind the three of them together, and she envied them.

When they stood on the upstairs landing Tom pointed to a door in front of them and ordered, 'In you go. There's an *en-suite* shower in the room if you need it, and various toiletries, all masculine, of course, but there, nevertheless.' He eyed her consideringly. 'Is there anything else I can get you?'

'No, thanks,' she told him, trying to match his impersonality, and thinking wryly that he'd only needed to have added the word 'madam' to that last question for her to have felt that a tip might be required.

'Unless, that is,' she said suddenly, with the devil driving her, 'you can suggest how I can make my hair less conspicuous. Maybe I should shave my head.'

'Don't be ridiculous!' he snapped. 'Your hair *is*—er—noticeable, but my comments were made only out of concern for. . .' he paused, and then said evenly, 'Port Health's reputation.'

That did it! Her hair wasn't attractive, or striking, or an unusual colour, it was merely noticeable, which could, of course, mean anything. Then, laying it on with a trowel, his concern had been only for Port Health. . .not *her*!

'I see!' she hissed angrily. 'So *that* was your concern. It makes me think that if *you* don't associate with women, you've no criticism of those of your sex who do. It doesn't matter what happens to me as long as it doesn't besmirch *your* excellence!'

She watched his face change. The polite mask had been replaced by rage.

'I've told you once already not to jump to conclusions about me, and you're doing it again! Assuming that my interest in your sex is nil or thereabouts, because I'm not constantly womanising, and because I take my commitment to my mother and Lucy seriously. How do *you* know what makes me tick, eh? You haven't known me for five minutes and you think you've got me all sussed out. . .an uppity young madam who is only too happy to sit in judgement on me, when she can't handle her own affairs.

'You're right about one thing, however. When it comes to most of the women I meet, I *don't* want to associate with them. It may be a case of once bitten twice shy, but let me tell you this. If I ever meet the woman who *is* right for me, she'll hear about it. In the meantime, let's see how a sexual drop-out like myself can put *you* right about one or two things.'

She listened to his angry tirade with a wide unblinking stare, aware that she'd really got under his skin this time. When he reached out for her and slammed her up against his chest, forcing her head back so that her lips were positioned for him to bend and take possession of her mouth with his, there was no fear in her, not with this man. Instead, there was excitement, desire, and triumph. Whatever the reason, she was in his arms, and he was kissing her with a slow possessive deliberation that was drawing the heart from out of her body, and turning her blood to fire.

Lucy's voice, coming from downstairs in the hallway, broke into the moment. She was bidding her grandmother goodnight, and Chloe wrenched herself out of his arms, swaying on her feet as she did so. As his hold fell away, the sensuous ache inside her was replaced with a bereft sort of emptiness, as if her body had been blessed, and then denied.

She groped for the door-handle and, as Lucy's feet came flying up the stairs, flung herself into the bedroom. Once the door was shut Chloe leaned against it, heart hammering, nerve-ends jagged with the sense of loss.

Chloe knew now why she couldn't get Tom Saracen out of her mind. The moment he'd pinned her to him, read the message of her eager mouth, and proceeded to answer it with an angry mocking reply of his own, she had known why Mike seemed insigificant, and why Saracen dominated her thoughts.

She was in love with a man who thought her an interfering busybody, and stupid with it, and he'd just dished up a disturbing portion of chastisement that had made her long for more.

As she lay in the bed that had been made up with the precision of a hospital orderly, her thoughts wouldn't let her sleep. She had been in the arms of two different men in one night. That alone was mind-bending, but the comparison between the two was indescribable. Now, in continuing amazement, she was trying to get her mind round the fact that she was sleeping in Tom's bed, in a tranquil house that was a far cry from the frippery and glitz of her own home. . . and, only a few yards away, lay the great canal, its still dark waters holding the spell that had brought him to her.

A tear rolled down her cheek as she wished they'd had a better start, that she had made a more lasting impression on him, displayed more maturity, and that there had been a less withdrawn approach on his part.

CHAPTER SIX

WHEN Chloe awoke the next morning she gazed around her, wide-eyed with the immediate recollection of where she was. The room was full of sunlight and a clear blue sky was visible through the window beside the bed.

Last night she'd been too wound up to take much notice of the room, but now in the bright light of day she observed Tom Saracen's bedroom, and decided that it was typical of the man. Clean, tidy, the décor in cool shades of ivory, with a few pieces of heavy walnut furniture. . .definitely a man's room. In her mother's eyes it would be akin to a prison cell with its lack of bows and bobs, but the absence of clutter appealed to Chloe. The room was like his life, cool, tidy, disciplined, and, whatever he had said last night, she was pretty sure *that* was how he liked it.

Her face burned as she thought back to how she'd goaded him into action, taunted him so that he'd forgotten his touch-me-not stance, and with what results! She knew that the episode on the boat would never be blotted from her memory, but neither would those exhilarating moments in Tom's arms. If his mother and Lucy hadn't been downstairs she had a feeling that it might have progressed from there.

But would it have? On his part, it was just an exercise in putting an 'uppity madam' in her place, and, as with everything else he did, he'd done it thoroughly.

She trailed her fingers along the crisp cotton sheets. Tom had given up his room for her, and his bed, but he'd taken away her serenity, her youthful confidence, and left her with what? Yearning?

But yearning wasn't *her* scene, was it? To have, or have not, was her philosophy, and from the way he'd dealt with her last night she'd like to bet that *he* was firmly slotted among the 'have not's of her life.

Sounds were drifting up through the open window, a man's deep tones and a woman's high laughter. Curious, she padded to the window in the voluminous pyjamas, and saw that although it was barely seven o'clock two people were already up and about.

Her host was standing by his garden gate holding the bridle of a frisky chestnut filly. That was surprising enough, but it was the 'filly' on the filly that had Chloe's eyes widening.

The rider had the curves of a mature woman. . .and the mannerisms. Her riding clothes didn't look as if they'd come off the peg at the local equestrian shop. They spoke of money, as did the huge solitaire diamond on her finger, glittering in the morning sun. Her hair was long and dark, cascading over her shoulders in shining waves.

Chloe couldn't hear what they were saying, but there was an easiness between them that dismayed her, that made her childish assumptions of the night before seem even more ridiculous.

Tom was the one who was laughing now, and the woman was glowing down on him with melting dark eyes. Chloe turned away. Whoever the woman was, he'd soon got to know her during the short time he'd been here, Chloe thought miserably, but then *she'd* only known him for a little while herself, and yet it had been long enough for her to fall in love with him.

The sound of muted music was coming from Lucy's room next door, and, remembering her promise of the previous night, she went and tapped on the door. Lucy was seated cross-legged on the floor in her pyjamas, and as Chloe went to squat beside her, she said eagerly, 'Shall I play the tape?'

'That's what I'm here for,' Chloe told her with a smile. 'For us to have our own little pop concert.'

Lucy giggled. 'You're nice, Chloe,' she said, and with sudden wistfulness, 'I wish. . .'

'What?' she asked gently. 'What do you wish?'

'I wish that Dad wasn't so friendly with the woman who lives next door,' she said awkwardly.

There was silence while Chloe digested that remark, and it was far from palatable. 'Does she ride?' she asked slowly.

Lucy nodded. 'You've seen her?' she asked.

'Yes. She and your father are chatting at the gate.'

Lucy nodded gloomily. 'That figures. We've only lived here a month, and from the very first day she's been around, offering us a meal on the day we moved in, asking if I'd like riding lessons. She owns the stables next door.'

'And so what's wrong with that?' Chloe questioned carefully. 'I imagine she's just trying to be neighbourly.'

'Yes, but she doesn't talk to Gran and me. It's only Dad she wants to see. Emily, our cleaner, who lives in the village, says that she's a wealthy widow looking for a husband.'

Chloe wished she'd stayed in her room. This was awful. She already had a rapport with Lucy, and the bond between them would be even stronger if they were going to be united in their dismay regarding the attractive horsewoman, but what would his daughter think if she discovered that their neighbour wasn't the only one who had designs on her father? In any case it would be most unfair to take sides.

'Maybe your father feels the need of the company of an attractive woman,' she said guardedly. . .rather than that of an 'uppity young madam' like herself!

'You mean he might want to get married again?' Lucy exclaimed in horror.

'One could hardly blame him if he did, could one?' Chloe pointed out reasonably, thinking that last night she'd had him down as a misogynist, and this morning she was labelling him the catch of the village. . .and hinting that he might be happy to be so described.

'No, I suppose not,' Lucy agreed slowly. 'But not to Chantal Mortimer! She's pushy and possessive. I'd be packed off to boarding-school before the confetti hit the ground.'

Chloe cuddled the child to her and said softly, 'Aren't we jumping the gun a bit? Your dad would never do anything to upset you or your grandma, and he can't know her all that well—there hasn't been time.'

'He took her to the theatre last Saturday,' Lucy persisted, 'and nobody makes Dad do anything he doesn't want to do. She came round at the beginning of the week waving tickets under his nose. Pretended that a friend had let her down, but I could tell by the gleam in her eye that it wasn't true.'

There wasn't a lot Chloe could say to that. The thought depressed her as much as it did Lucy. She decided that it was time to change the subject, and it wasn't all for Lucy's benefit when she said gently, 'Tell me about your mother? What was she like?'

'I can't remember her very well,' Lucy said slowly, 'but I do recall that she had hair the same colour as yours.'

Chloe's spirits took a dive. So not only were she and the dead Herta women of the water, but the Dutch woman had been fair like herself, which was not altogether surprising, she supposed, considering the country of her origin. But taking it all round, it was a fact that wasn't going to increase her standing with doubting Thomas.

'So what's going on here?' his voice asked suddenly from the doorway. They hadn't heard him come in because of the music, and as the two young pyjama-clad figures turned to face him Chloe felt that she must look like a picked bone in the sloppy pyjamas after the voluptuous Chantal.

Getting hastily to her feet, she clutched the lapels of the jacket together and told him, 'We were having our own little pop concert.'

'So it would seem,' he said drily, but his mouth was soft and his eyes less guarded, as they always were when Lucy was around. How he was feeling towards herself this morning after his outburst and subsequent savage passion of the night before, she couldn't begin to guess, but he seemed pleasant enough. Maybe it was the moments he had just spent with his neighbour that had mellowed him.

'If you want to get dressed I'll get some breakfast going,' he told her. 'Mother has hers on a tray in her room, and so does this young lady, so it will be just you and I à la kitchen table.'

'That will be fine,' Chloe agreed hurriedly, edging towards the door while adjusting to the fact that it was going to be a cosy twosome for breakfast, which was the last thing she was geared for this morning.

When she went downstairs it was 'The Big Breakfast Show' in the kitchen—fresh orange juice, cereal, egg with crispy bacon, and toast to follow—and when she protested that tea and toast would have been enough Tom commanded, 'Save your breath, Chloe, and eat,' and, because it all looked very appetising and she was hungry, she obeyed.

'That was delicious,' she said sincerely when they'd eaten, 'but I really do feel that I'm being a nuisance.'

'You are,' he told her calmly, 'but you would have been more of a nuisance in the empty flat in Manchester. At least while I've got you under scrutiny your nuisance value isn't increasing.'

'I imagine that it was at its peak last night?' she said rashly.

'You *could* say that,' he agreed blandly, 'but I think we cleared the air, don't you?'

He had a nerve! But as the bright colour came up in her face the words didn't come as swiftly to her tongue. She felt there was nothing she could say that wouldn't give her away, that wouldn't tell him how much his kiss and the magical contact that went with it had meant to her.

The sensible thing to do was change the subject, and she did so by saying, 'If you'd take me to where I left the bike I'd like to go home to change my clothes. I know it will make me late at the office, but. . .'

'By all means go home,' he said immediately. 'It's daylight now, which is more than it was when you wanted to go home in your overwrought state last night. I'll wait for you in the office, and once you get back we'll get the day's duties under way.'

There was no sign of Lorraine when Chloe got back to the flat. When she checked her mother's bedroom the bed hadn't been slept in, which usually meant that Lorraine had stayed out late and slept at a friend's house. It was a room feminine in the extreme, with a peach satin canopy over the bed and matching sheets, and as she prepared to pull the door closed behind her Chloe thought with amusement of how it differed from the room *she'd* used the previous night.

She stopped. Something had caught her eye. An expensive wig that her mother sometimes wore was languishing in long dark silkiness on its stand by the dressing-table. She went across and picked it up, eyeing it thoughtfully, and then she placed it on her head. Gone was the pale gold bob, and in its place a hairpiece that was as near to the hair of the woman on the chestnut horse as she would ever get.

A wicked little smile curved around her lips. Thomas didn't approve of her hair, for what might be more than one reason, so she was dutifully going to obey his instructions and keep it out of sight, and if he didn't like the way of it. . .too bad.

Obviously she couldn't wear the wig under her

helmet so it went into one of the panniers on the bike, and the moment she got to the office she slipped into the ladies' room and put it on.

The effect was startling to say the least. The wig's long seductive curls were definitely not her style, and the extreme fairness of her skin looked like a death mask against the black tresses, but she wasn't going to chicken out. The dark prince of the canal was in for a shock.

When she popped her head round the door of the outer office Maureen goggled.

'Chloe!' she gasped. 'Is it really you?'

'Of course it is,' she grinned. 'I've been ticked off for flashing my hair, so I thought I would subdue it.'

'Subdue it!' the other woman hooted. 'You look. . . weird!'

'Where is our lord and master?' she hissed.

'Down at one of the quays. Some problem with a broken seal on a food container. He left a message for you to stay put until he gets back.'

'Oh, I will,' she said with mock fervour. 'I wouldn't dream of going anywhere until I've had his opinion on my new look.'

When she heard his car stop outside Chloe bent over the filing cabinet, with her back to the door, and within seconds he was bounding up the stairs and breezing into the office.

She was aware that he'd stopped, and there was silence for a few moments, until he said coldly, 'Excuse me. You may be wearing Port Health uniform, but what are you doing in my office?'

'I'm doing my job,' she said airily as she turned to face him, and in that fragment of time she knew that if she died on the spot she would die happy because of the look on his face.

His jaw had dropped and he was screwing his eyes up as if unable to credit what he saw, and then he said in a horrified whisper, 'You must be crazy! You've dyed your hair!'

She laughed. He really must be flabbergasted, or it would have dawned on him immediately that her own hair wasn't as long as that of the wig, but he was rallying quickly, blue eyes glittering with what she hoped was amusement, but feared might be annoyance.

'Take it off!' he snapped. 'You want your behind smacking! I can't say one word to you but what you have to turn it into a book. Where did you get it?'

'It belongs to my mother,' she said meekly, moving her head from side to side so that the long black swath of hair swung provocatively on her shoulders. 'When I saw it, there seemed to be a solution being offered to me with regard to the problem of my hair.'

'Either *you* take it off. . .or *I* will,' he gritted through clenched teeth, 'and when you've returned to your normal appearance maybe we can get some work done.

'During the past week the importers have sent us bills of lading with regard to shipments that have arrived at the Port of Manchester this morning, and it's our job to see that all the seals are intact on the containers from the EEC countries, and do a sample check on the nuts and fishmaws that have come from the Americas. They are always suspect, and if we've any doubts we'll bung them to the public analyst.

'We've also had a message from the port where it has docked previously that one of the vessels on today's list might have tried to repair a faulty refrigerated container. It wasn't functioning while they were there, so obviously the temperatures will have dropped. The authorities had a hunch that the crew might have tried to fix it which, of course, just won't do from a health and safety point of view.'

Chloe had removed the wig and was flicking a comb through her own hair as she said, 'What are fishmaws?'

'Dried fish bladders. They're used for finings for beer, and if you've quite finished we'll get moving.'

'Yes, Cap'n,' she said, with the devil still in her.

He glared at her.

'It's quite obvious that you've soon got over last night's ordeal.'

'Which one?' she questioned innocently, and was ashamed to see a shadow cross his face.

'Both of them, by the looks of it,' he said grimly as he held the door for her to go through.

Chloe's keen eyes found mould when she took a random sample from the brazil nuts that were awaiting their inspection on the quayside, and she immediately put them to one side for the public analyst. She had learned during her training that there was always a danger of aflatoxin being found in stored nuts, or grain, or suchlike, and that it was a very dangerous form of mould that appeared on the food after flies had been on it. She had also learned that it was judged to be the cause of the high incidence of liver cancer in tropical Africa.

Thomas had gone to one of the other docks to check if the crew of the ship with the faulty refrigerated container had been doing a DIY job on it during the trip from their last port of call, and when he came back an hour later it was to inform her that the vigilance of the officers at the other port, though exemplary, had on this occasion been mistaken. The container was not in use.

When she told him about the mould he said immediately, 'Good for you. Lots of eyes would have missed it as the quantity is so small, but that's what we're here for. . .to spot the health hazards that might be missed and because of that passed on to the public.'

'There's a container over there that looks a bit battered,' she pointed out. 'Do you think we should ask the dockers to open it?'

'Yes, of course,' he agreed. 'We. . .that is, you and I, are not going to leave anything to chance. If there is ever the slightest doubt about anything connected with Port Health in your mind. . .check it out. It might be obvious, or just the result of a hunch, but do it.'

The fishmaws inside the battered container appeared to be in good condition, but she sent a sample for analysing just the same, and then resealed all the containers that had been opened with a new seal of her own.

'We'll have the results back in forty-eight hours,' he said, 'and if there *is* aflatoxin it will show that we're on the ball, but the importers won't be too chuffed when we notify them that they've got a dodgy cargo on their hands.'

They were on the quayside most of the day, and when it was time to go home Chloe said carefully, 'About Thursday?'

He swivelled to face her.

'Yes?'

'I feel that you and your family have seen quite enough of me after accommodating me last night.'

'Why not let us be the judge of that?' he countered. 'The invitation for tomorrow comes from my mother, not me, and she will be disappointed if you don't come. She is no mean cook and likes nothing better than to have visitors.'

'Even under last night's conditions?' she questioned.

'Did you hear her complaining?'

'No, but. . .what about her leg? Doesn't she get very tired?'

'Sometimes, but Lucy and I are always there to help. She's worn the brace a long time. The injury was from a car accident.'

'I see.'

'So we'll expect you as arranged,' he said, in a tone that seemed to say. . .'Stop prevaricating!'

It had been a satisfying day, Chloe decided as she let herself into the flat. After her late start and the episode of the wig, she and Tom had worked together in harmony as they performed the functions of Port Health.

There had been no mishaps, no more bad vibes, just two people doing the job they were paid to do, and it had made the happenings of the night before less traumatic.

All the time they had been working he had been instructing her in the job. He had warned her that although ships with rats on board were rare, it didn't follow that there wouldn't come a day when she might find herself faced with a very unpleasant task.

He had also put her in the picture regarding the other side of the coin, explaining about the really big ships that came to the docks, and how, in spite of most of them being oil transporters, they were palatial inside, with their own swimming pool, gymnasium, and hospital wings.

'I'd like to go on one of those,' she had said immediately.

'Yes, I thought you might,' he'd acknowledged drily, 'and as it happens I know the captain of one of them. It's a Dutch ship called the *Scandar*. I believe he frequently docks at Stanlow, so the next time he comes I'll take you on board for lunch.'

'Shall I wear the wig?' she had teased, and that time he'd played along with her.

'Hardly. Scandinavian women are notoriously fair. You won't make heads turn on any of *their* vessels.'

'In that case, maybe I *had* better wear it,' she had suggested.

'I wouldn't recommend it,' he'd told her. 'It doesn't do anything for you.'

She had put her hand up to her own hair.

'And this does?'

His eyes had been watchful, and his voice had roughened as he had answered the question.

'Of course it does. . .as you are well aware.'

And that friendly enough exchange of words had been the only time they had got on to personal matters.

Today her mother was home when Chloe got in, a happening that of late was rare. She wasn't alone, from the sound of it, as voices were coming from the sitting-room. When she went in Lorraine was chatting to a big grey-haired man in a light beige suit. When Lorraine saw Chloe standing there she exclaimed absently, 'Oh! Chloe!' as if the fact that she had a

daughter had just dawned on her. 'This is Edgar. . .
Edgar Harkness,' she said, without her usual petu-
lance. 'From New York.' Turning to the man, who
was watching them both with a relaxed smile, she said,
'This is my daughter, Chloe, Edgar. I think I might
have mentioned her.'

Big deal! Chloe thought. It was clear that *her* name
didn't crop up very often in her mother's conversation!

'Nice to meet you, Chloe,' he said in a deep nasal
drawl as he shook her warmly by the hand. Chloe had
the feeling that this man wasn't just one of her
mother's usual hangers on. . .he was different. There
was an air of jocular competence about him that spoke
of power and money, without it being unpleasant, and
incredibly her mother seemed docile in his presence,
doting almost. Her next words confirmed that they
weren't newly acquainted.

'Edgar goes back to the States at the end of the
month, and he's asked me to go with him for a
holiday,' she said skittishly.

'You too, my dear, if you want to,' he said gallantly,
but Lorraine wasn't having that.

'Chloe has a job. She's only just started it. An
extended vacation wouldn't be possible.'

'Is that so?' he said easily. 'And what do you do?'

Lorraine shuddered. 'She works on the canal. . .the
grubby Manchester Ship Canal.'

He obviously didn't share her mother's distaste.
'You do! I'd planned on seeing that while I've been
over here, but the time has flown.'

Chloe was aware that since walking into the room
she hadn't been able to get in a word, not through any
fault of their visitor, and she'd had just about enough.

'I'm sure that from my mother's description of my employment you could be excused for thinking that maybe I was a docker, or a deckhand on a dredger, but the truth of it is that I'm employed in Port Health, as an environmental health officer.'

'Say! That sure sounds interesting.'

'Yes, it is,' Chloe told him with a smile, and thought he'd no idea just how interesting it really was, but that was partly due to working with a man called Tom Saracen.

On Thursday afternoon the two Port Health officers boarded a pleasure boat anchored in a marina on the Weaver, and once again Chloe was enchanted by the beauty of the river and its surroundings.

'We're here to do the yearly inspection for the registration of food premises,' her companion told the captain, 'and as you can see we're both new to the river. I'm Tom Saracen, and this is my assistant, Chloe Cavendish.'

As the captain, an amiable middle-aged man in a navy jersey and a knitted woollen hat, shook hands and invited them to go ahead, she was intrigued to see how spacious and well organised was his boat.

Seeing her expression, the captain said, 'We can take up to a hundred passengers and six crew.'

There was a bar at one end, and a small galley with a stainless-steel sink, next to a shelf for storing pots and glasses, and further along was a refrigerated area for storing drinks.

As he looked around him, keen blue eyes missing nothing, Tom said, 'I see that you have no facilities for preparing food here. What sort of an arrangement do you have?'

'We have a contract with an hotel by the side of the river,' the captain said quickly. 'They bring whatever food we order and take back all the dishes. That way there is no clutter.'

'Is it brought on board in insulated containers?' he questioned.

'Yes.'

'And what about the waste?'

'It goes into a special tank where it is treated and is then pumped ashore.'

Tom nodded. 'That sounds all right, then. What about hot water?'

'We have an excellent geyser,' the captain replied.

'Do you serve tea and coffee as well as alcohol?'

'Yes, we can cope with that.'

After they had scrutinised the bar area carefully and noted that it was clean and uncluttered, Tom announced, 'We'll see the toilets next.'

When they went into the first of the two small compartments Chloe saw that it was served with a foot pump, and she asked curiously, 'What sort of an arrangement have you got here? Am I right in presuming that the waste goes into a holding tank?'

Tom nodded his approval of her grasp of the situation as the captain replied, 'Yes, that's correct.'

'And that it's fitted with a deodoriser?' she persisted.

'Yes,' he confirmed again, 'and the flushing equipment, clear water, comes from the main holding tank next to it.'

'That seems to be satisfactory enough,' Tom said in his usual crisp fashion. 'Now, what about safety?'

They were on the bottom deck where chairs and tables were screwed down in front of the bar area, and windows on all sides offered travellers an excellent view of the river.

'The life raft is over there,' the captain said, pointing to a brightly painted example of the equipment in question, 'and we're in touch with the lockmaster at all times during sailing. We have to notify him how many we have on board every time, in case of an emergency.'

'What sort of trade do you do?' Chloe asked. 'Is it just pleasure trips up and down the river?'

'Some,' he agreed. 'We have weekend cruises with a folk group on board, but a lot of our business comes from private parties. James Hanbury, who was the previous chief port health officer, had his ruby wedding celebration on board. He thought it seemed only fitting.'

She nodded, impressed with the idea. It would be nice to have a wedding reception on the riverboat, but as her imagination began to run riot she was brought down to earth by Tom Saracen saying decisively, 'Right. Everything seems to be in order. Thanks for your co-operation.'

As they drove back to Port House Tom remarked, 'I shouldn't think our predecessors had much trouble with that guy. He knows his stuff, and his record over the years is good.'

'Mmm,' she murmured, still bemused with the idea of sitting in a launch sailing down the Weaver, dressed in a wedding gown, with smiling guests following on behind. The only snag to that dream, which wasn't the kind of thing she usually dreamed about, or hadn't been until lately, was that there was one vital commodity missing. . .a bridegroom. She had a feeling that there was no chance of a volunteer emerging from present company.

But, having said that, was that what she wanted? She glanced quickly at his dark profile, the mouth that rarely smiled, the tight jawline, and knew that it was. To be able to make him happy and carefree, wrapped around with her own brand of uncomplicated love, and to be able to tell him truthfully that there would be love to spare for Lucy, too, was a glimpse of a paradise that she doubted she would ever see.

He was eyeing her curiously. 'I can almost hear the wheels turning inside that head of yours,' he said in his usual dry manner. 'What is it that you're pondering?'

'I was thinking how romantic it would be to have one's wedding reception on a pleasure boat on the Weaver,' she told him, in an abbreviated version of the truth.

His eyes darkened and he was nibbling his lip with even white teeth. She thought that there wasn't going to be any comment, but she was wrong.

'Why? Are *you* thinking of dabbling in what can be a very precarious way of life?' he asked casually. 'The boyfriend who took you out last Saturday, maybe?'

'No, of course not,' she said with equal sang-froid. 'He was just one of the gang from the bike club. I'm quite happy as I am.' Which was true up to a point. With Tom Saracen's distrust of the fair sex, which had once again been evident in his description of the married state, she had a feeling that this was about as happy as she was likely to get.

CHAPTER SEVEN

'You're all geared up for this evening, then?' Tom asked when they got back to the office.

'Yes. I've brought a change of clothes with me,' Chloe told him. 'Dining with you and your family will make a pleasant start to the Easter weekend.'

'What have you got planned?' he wanted to know. 'Will your mother be at home?'

Chloe laughed wryly.

'I don't know. Probably not, as I think she's found herself a man friend.'

'Really?'

'Yes. She's met a wealthy American, who owns a soft-drinks company in the States. He's invited her to stay with him when he goes back at the end of the month. Whether she'll be spending Easter with him, I really don't know. For once, she seems happy and I'm glad for her.'

He was eyeing her thoughtfully.

'And will she be considering you when she makes her plans?'

'I doubt it,' Chloe told him with reluctant honesty, 'but I don't mind. I'm used to our way of life, though, having said that, it doesn't stop me from envying you yours.'

'Mine!' he exclaimed. 'There's nothing exciting about *my* life.'

'I meant because you are a close family.'

'Yes, I see what you mean,' he agreed gravely, 'but close families don't appear out of the blue, Chloe; one has to work at it.'

'Perhaps you think I haven't tried hard enough?' she questioned.

'No. I didn't say that,' he protested. 'I would imagine that you're pretty easy to live with. Your mother appears to be the one at fault from where I'm standing. Is she insecure?'

'Yes, you could say that, I suppose. It doesn't stop me from being fond of her, you know, but there are times when I wish we were closer. I got on best with my dad, like Lucy does with you. When he died, I was very lonely, as my mother doesn't seem to be able to give affection.'

Chloe felt that they had discussed her family life, or the lack of it, for long enough. She didn't want Tom to think she was looking for a chance to cry on his shoulder, and so she said, 'You were asking what I've got planned for Easter?'

He nodded.

'I'm going for a run with the bike club tomorrow, and on Saturday I'm going to do some shopping. Lucy can come with me, if you like. . .and if *she* likes.'

'Are you sure?' he said, eyeing her doubtfully. 'It doesn't mean that because you work with me you have to be nursemaid to my daughter.'

'I know that,' she told him laughingly, 'but I don't mind showing her the north, honestly.'

'In that case, I'll put the offer to her, or better still ask her yourself tonight. She'll appreciate it more coming straight from you.'

'OK,' she agreed easily, and would have left it at that.

He still had his mind on her home life and wanted to know, 'What would you do if your mother remarried?'

'I wouldn't play gooseberry, that's for sure,' she told him firmly. 'I'd get myself a small flat, overlooking the Weaver preferably.'

'That river really gets to you, doesn't it?'

'Yes, it does,' she admitted. 'It's beautiful.'

'You're a very uncomplicated person,' he said sombrely. 'Although it would appear that you *do* have three loves, and not many women of your age can lay claim to that.'

Chloe became very still. What was that supposed to mean? 'I'm not with you,' she told him, half laughing. 'What are they?'

'An industrial waterway, a picturesque river. . .and, wait for it. . .an urban street tiger!'

Should she tell him that he'd miscounted, she wondered, that she had four loves, one of them very new, and it was the most important one? Hardly. Not unless she wanted to ruin the evening before it had begun.

'That makes me sound rather weird,' she said in mock protest.

Tom shook his head and said, 'Not weird. . . unusual, maybe, but what's wrong with being different?'

'Nothing, I suppose,' she agreed awkwardly. But she wasn't different really, was she? She had done what thousands of women before her had done—fallen in love with her boss. *That* was the love he hadn't mentioned, but then he wouldn't, as he didn't know anything about it.

'Do you mind if I get changed at your house?' she asked as they packed up for the night. 'The clothes I've brought are hardly suitable for riding the bike in.'

'Yes, of course,' he agreed. 'Lucy is intending to impress you with a new outfit. I think it's what they call the Oxfam look, a seersucker blouse, long frayed cardigan, and a hobble skirt, and on her feet the coal barges that seem to be so popular with young girls.'

Chloe laughed as he let out a long sigh. 'If it makes her happy, so what? She's lovely.'

'You really think so?' he asked with an anxiety foreign to him.

'Yes, I do,' she said firmly, and had a sudden urge to warn him of his daughter's fears regarding their glamorous neighbour, but she held back. The last two days there had been peace between them, a camaraderie that came from accepting each other for what they were, of working together in a common cause, and she didn't want to spoil it. There was no telling what kind of an interpretation he might put on that sort of warning, and she decided that for the time being it must be left unsaid.

Almost from the moment of meeting Tom Saracen she had wanted to show him that she wasn't all crash helmet, leather jacket and waxed trousers, and tonight, on the eve of Easter, she was going to accomplish it.

With her extremely fair colouring, Chloe was aware that she looked good in pastel shades, but she could also wear black with great success, and so tonight it was going to be the little black number that all the jokes were about. The dress that every woman should have to fall back on in their wardrobe, for the occasion when they wanted to look smart and seductive.

It was made out of wool crêpe, with a scooped-out neckline, three-quarter sleeves and a full skirt, and to go with it she had brought sheer stockings and high-heeled black shoes, having decided that the only thing to relieve the outfit was going to be large pearl clusters for her ears.

The effect was to make her look older and more sophisticated, and as she eyed herself in the mirror in Lucy's bedroom her young hostess said, 'You look. . . er. . .'

'What?' she asked doubtfully.

'Nearly as old as Chantal.'

Chloe pulled a face and then started to laugh, and after a moment Lucy joined in, aware that it had been a backhanded compliment. When at last they subsided Chloe wheezed, 'Thanks a bunch! Maybe I should change back into my bike gear!' and that started them off again.

Mrs Saracen was in the kitchen presiding over the oven and a collection of pans that were giving off appetising smells. When Chloe appeared in the doorway she paused from her labours to say warmly, 'You look very lovely, my dear.'

'Thank you,' Chloe said, 'but I do feel that I'm putting you to an awful lot of trouble. What can I do to help?'

'Nothing. Help yourself to a sherry, while I check to see if the duck is done, and perhaps you could keep an eye open for Tom and our other guest. He's just gone to fetch her.'

Chloe's spirits plummeted. So she wasn't the only person who had been invited to dinner. When Lucy said gloomily from behind, 'I would have thought she knew the way. She's here often enough!' Chloe felt that the evening was already spoilt.

Chantal Mortimer was linked to him as they came through the patio window, her hand tucked possessively in the crook of his arm. Chloe's eyes narrowed. What had happened to Mr Touch-me-not? It looked as if the exclusion zone didn't apply to madame from next door, but the next moment she'd got herself in hand.

An unexpected though passionate embrace didn't give her a prior claim on Tom Saracen. The incident had been staged to teach her a lesson, and it had certainly done that. It had taught her that here was a man she could love with all her heart. Sombre, prickly sometimes, but physically very attractive, mentally with a mind like a rapier, and morally living his life to a pattern, a pattern that the fates and a blonde Dutch sea captain had mapped out for him. He was bound by it, at least as far as *she* was concerned. It remained to be seen what set of rules he was going to produce for his friendship with Chantal Mortimer.

It seemed that the lady had some rules of her own and they weren't quite what Chloe was expecting. When Chantal had unhooked herself from Tom and he had introduced her to Chloe, Chantal told her charmingly, 'I'm so lucky to have such nice neighbours. This house had been empty for a long time and I was dreading who might buy it, but my worries are over. I have Tom, Lucy and Grace Saracen next door to me, and am thankful.'

'Yes, I'm sure that it must be a relief to you,' Chloe said politely as she tried to get the measure of the attractive widow.

For the first few moments after he had brought Chantal into the room the only thing Chloe had been aware of was Tom's eyes upon herself, standing there in the black dress, like Cinderella at the ball, only on this occasion it wasn't rags that she had cast aside for finery, but her Port Health uniform.

His head had jerked up and his lips parted in surprise when he saw her, but it had seemed to Chloe that she was overshadowed by the vision beside him in an emerald-green trouser suit with lots of expensive jewellery. Now that same vision was chatting to her with a bouncy sort of friendliness that was quite disarming.

'She's trying to win you over,' Lucy said in a whisper as they all went into the dining-room. 'Next thing you know she'll be asking you to be a bridesmaid!'

Chloe gave her a quick squeeze and murmured in return, 'I haven't formed an opinion yet, but Chantal seems very nice. Are you sure that you're not being too hard on her? And the last thing your father would want is *me* for a bridesmaid. He sees enough of me at work!' As they seated themselves around a beautifully laid table she was making a mental correction. A bridesmaid was the *next* to the last thing he would want. The *last* thing he'd want would be to have her as a *bride*!

The meal was delicious, with sardines in a wine sauce for starters, followed by mushroom soup, and then came the duck in orange sauce with crisp fresh vegetables. Tom's mother served up lemon sorbet for dessert, and when finally they gathered in the drawing-room for coffee, and Chloe thanked her softly for an excellent meal, she felt tears threaten to choke her. It was at times like these, in the midst of somebody else's family, that she realised what she was missing.

'It was my pleasure, Chloe,' Grace said as they sat together on the sofa. 'I love cooking, and once the meal is served my work is done. Tom and Lucy always do the washing-up.' She indicated their departing backs. 'That's where they'll be off to now, and I believe that Chantal has popped back home as she's expecting a phone call.

'I've been wanting to ask you how you're enjoying the job,' Grace went on. 'I believe that you're not long out of college.'

'I love it,' she said without hesitation.

'And how do you get on with my son?'

'Er—very well. . .I think, although that is just my opinion. He may think otherwise.'

'If that is the case, I haven't heard him say so,' Grace said with a twinkly smile.

'Yes, well, he tells me that he never discusses his staff with anyone, so maybe. . .?'

'I don't think so,' his mother chided gently. 'But tell me about your family, and where you live.'

'There is just my mother and me,' Chloe said tranquilly, her earlier moment of anguish under control. 'My father died when I was the same age as Lucy. He had a company on the Ship Canal, which was the start of its fascination for me.'

'You know that Tom's wife was in shipping?' Grace asked.

'Yes, he told me,' Chloe said quietly. 'It must have been a very sad time for you all.'

'It was, most of all for him. He gave up the sea for Lucy's sake, even though it was in his blood. But in Herta's case I don't think there was any blood. It was pure salt water.'

'Did she have any family?' Chloe asked, knowing that it was something she'd been curious about from the start. . .whether there were any Dutch grandparents.

'Her mother died shortly after Herta and Tom were married, but at the time she was killed her father and brother were alive, running the company. The shock caused her father to have a stroke and he passed away soon after, and now it is her brother who runs the family business. . .Lucy's uncle.'

'Where is Chantal?' Tom's voice said from the doorway, putting an end to the conversation.

'Gone home to take a phone call that she's expecting,' his mother informed him.

'Is she coming back?'

Chloe squirmed in her seat. He was piling the agony on. The next thing he would be going in search of her, but she was mistaken.

'Would you like to go for a sail?' he asked of her.

'Me?' she asked in surprise.

He eyed her with raised brows. 'There are only three of us in the room at this moment, and I know that a sail at this time of night is not my mother's idea of heaven, so, yes, the invitation is aimed at yourself. It's quite mild out there tonight.'

It was her turn to be sceptical. 'What in?' she asked doubtfully.

'I have a rowing boat tied up at the back of the house.'

She looked down at the dress. . .and the high-heeled shoes. . .and shook her head. 'I don't think so.'

He was laughing and his mother joined in.

'He's teasing,' she said. 'We have no rowing boat.'

'So what, then?' Chloe asked uneasily, with the feeling that he might just be getting his own back over the wig episode.

He wasn't prepared to enlighten her. 'Have you got a jacket?' he asked.

'Er—yes.'

'Right. Be sure to bring it with you, and. . .no more questions. . .all will shortly be revealed.'

'I hope it's not a rubber dinghy!'

'Wait and see,' he commanded, and led the way to the car.

'I thought we were going for a sail?' she questioned.

'We are, but we've got to get to cast-off point first.'

'Doesn't Lucy want to come?' she asked, playing for time because she wasn't sure what she was letting herself in for.

'She hasn't been asked. I was intending taking Chantal and yourself, but as she seems to have disappeared it looks like being just the two of us.'

So it wasn't a one-to-one invitation, Chloe thought prosaically. The lady from next door would have been included if she hadn't disappeared, but Chloe supposed there was a grain of comfort in the fact that he hadn't insisted on her presence.

When they set off he pointed the car towards Ellesmere Port and she eyed him in puzzlement, but didn't speak. It would be time enough to say her piece when they got to wherever they were going.

Tom stopped the car at the marina where the boat museum was situated, and pointed to a smart new launch moored beside the other craft. 'There she is! What do you think?'

Chloe could just about make it out in the spring dusk, and, turning to him in surprise, she said, 'I think I'd like to know what's going on. Who does the launch belong to?'

He sighed, as if he couldn't credit her having to ask. 'Me, of course.'

'You?' she echoed.

'Yep. It was delivered earlier in the week. I've tried it out a couple of times and it's great.'

'You've been on the canal in it?'

'Sure. As long as I keep in touch with port control by radio with regard to my movements, I shan't be treading on anyone's toes, like, for example, the local authorities or the Ship Canal Co. Obviously port control need to know where I am when I'm using it, in case any large vessels are coming my way, as I could be overturned in the wash as they go by. And, that being so, I'm going to check with them now, to make sure it's OK to take her out on the canal.' He jumped down into the boat and held out his arms. 'Are you coming? I know it's not the Weaver, but any port in a storm.'

She started to laugh. 'The port in question being Ellesmere? And please don't mention storms. I'm not dressed for bad weather.'

His arms were still held out invitingly, to catch her as she jumped down. She knew if she hesitated any longer he might guess how his touch affected her. So, clutching the high-heeled shoes in her hand so as not to damage the deck, she stepped into his arms with as much grace as she could muster, making the most out of the brief moment of contact.

It wasn't as brief as she had expected. He held her to him for a few seconds, searching her eyes in the dim lighting, and then said, to her astonishment, 'You look very beautiful and much older in the black dress.'

Chloe gazed back at him. 'Actually I *do* feel much older, but it's not because of the black dress.'

'What's the reason, then?'

She could hear the water lapping against the sides of the boat in the silence that followed his question, and a ship's hooter sounded eerily from near by. It was the moment to tell him the truth. . .that she felt older because she had shed her youthful cocoon after those moments in his arms on the landing outside his bedroom. She had become a woman in every sense of the word. A woman in love.

But it was too risky to tell him the truth. If he laughed at her, or reverted back to his misogynist role, she would want to shrivel up. So she eased herself reluctantly out of his arms and said carelessly, 'It must be the job, the responsibility of keeping the port and the eight riparian boroughs healthy.'

He stared at her for a moment as if she puzzled him, and then turned his attention to the radio. As he confirmed with port control that it was safe for him to take the launch out for a brief sail as there were no large vessels in the vicinity, Chloe went to stand by the bows.

She shivered. It was getting cooler, but she wanted

to avoid putting on her jacket. Tom had said she looked beautiful in the black dress, and so the longer it was on view, the longer he would have to admire her in it.

As the engine spluttered into life Chloe turned to face him, the light from the marina and a scudding moon throwing her hair and the whiteness of her throat into relief against the darkness of the dress.

There was exaltation on his face and contentment, too, and she wondered if this was how he had looked when he'd sailed his own ship, before he had become a land-bound widower. There was sea salt in *his* blood, too, but, unlike that of his wife, it was tempered with tenderness, the tenderness he felt for his child. Fond as she was of Lucy, in that moment Chloe could only envy her.

'Come and stand by me,' Tom commanded as the launch nosed its way noisily into the canal, 'so that we can sail our waterway together.' Laughter rumbled in his throat. 'Past the oil tanks and the refineries, the chemical plants and the scrubland that borders its banks. No swan, heron, or gleaming wild mink here, but beautiful, none the less, in its divine usefulness.'

Tears stung her eyes as she moved towards him. He was right. The Weaver and the Ship Canal were so different, but each was beautiful in its own way, and as his arm went around her, and the launch cut its way through the dark glistening water, his contentment washed over her, and she was happy just to be close to him.

They seemed to have been sailing forever beneath the moonlit sky, when suddenly everything was blotted out and they were in fog. Thick and damp, it enclosed them like a grey woollen shroud.

'Damn! Where has this come from?' he muttered, removing his arm from around her shoulders. 'Check with port control, Chloe. Ask them how far it stretches. Give them our position and ask what they advise.'

'They say there's a lay-by a hundred yards further on,' she told him a few seconds later. 'and that we should stay in it until the mist clears. The land is marshy here-abouts, and it can cause bad visibility, but they reckon that most of the mist is coming from the Mersey. All shipping in this area has been advised to stay put.'

When he had steered them carefully into the lay-by Tom said, 'This is a turn-up for the book! We're out here without food or heat, and it's getting colder by the minute. I haven't had time to stock up with food yet—there seemed to be no rush—but I should have remembered that the weather has a sense of humour all of its own.'

'Maybe it will soon clear,' Chloe said optimistically as they sat in the small cabin and the thick grey mass swirled around the launch. She'd had to put her jacket on or freeze, and when he saw her shiver Tom reached for a heavy quilted jacket of his own out of one of the cupboards. So much for glamour, she thought wryly as he insisted that she put it on.

'We could be here for hours, you know,' he warned, and she smiled to herself as she envisaged his expression if she were to say 'Good!'.

The fates were on her side tonight. She was alone with Tom Saracen, admittedly in a less than idyllic setting, but alone with him nevertheless, without Chantal, the beautiful widow. A threesome in these conditions would hardly have been a laugh a minute, and with that thought in mind she said, 'How do you think Chantal would have felt if she'd been marooned in the fog with us?'

He gave his dry laugh. 'Completely cheesed off. She goes in for comfort with a capital "C". My comely neighbour is not cut out for discomfort. Gin and tonics, satin pyjamas and diamonds are her life's blood.'

Chloe chose to ignore the remark about the pyjamas, as a query regarding them might receive an unwanted answer, but she was prepared to question the rest.

'You say that she's all for comfort? I wouldn't say being on horseback at seven o'clock in the morning was the behaviour of a comfort-seeker.'

'*That* is connected with money. Most people will get up off their butt when there's some of it to be had.'

'I'm not with you,' she said.

'Riding lessons. She doesn't give them, her staff do that, but she's wise enough to know that it pays to keep a finger on the pulse.'

'I see,' she said thoughtfully.

He was eyeing her speculatively in the dim light, and when he said with a frayed smile, 'What shall we talk about?' she countered back promptly,

'Waste.'

The word revealed what was in her mind, because it *was* a waste, the two of them out here in the shrouded mist making polite conversation. They could be in each other's arms, kissing, whispering endearments, making love. . .

'Waste?' he echoed, as if she'd gone out of her mind. . .and maybe she had. 'What sort of waste?'

'Waste as with regard to Port Health,' she said with a quickly assumed efficiency. 'I've seen the skips on the quayside, and am aware that they are for ships' waste, and are emptied promptly into special tips, but what about the big vessels? There was one in Ellesmere Port as we passed, a huge thing. How does that size of ship get rid of its waste? If it's not dealt with speedily it can be a health hazard, as we both know.'

'I don't believe I'm hearing this,' he said slowly. 'It has its own incinerator, as I'm sure you're well aware, and why in the name of glory are we on that subject? We're supposed to be off duty!'

'Because it's less dangerous than some,' she replied lightly.

'Oh, yes? And what *are* the dangerous subjects?'

He'd got to his feet and was standing over her.

'I'm waiting for an answer, Chloe.'

He was so near that his breath fanned her cheek, and her fingers ached to reach up and touch the dark face above hers. There was a sweet melting sensation in her bones and cruising butterflies in her stomach.

Throwing caution to the winds, she said, 'They're the ones that increase my awareness of you to such an extent that my brain seizes up. . .I can't think straight, and that's not the way I usually am. Normally I'm cool, uncomplicated and unruffled, but not when you're around.'

'Is that so?' he breathed softly. 'And how do you expect me to react to that amazing statement?'

'I don't know,' she told him as their eyes held. 'I really don't know.'

'Well, *I* do,' he said in the same hushed tone. 'Kiss

me, Chloe. Prove to me that what you've just said is true.'

She reached up and cupped his face in her hands, pulling it down towards her parted lips as she did so, then kissed him lightly on the mouth.

His arms were round her now, his body hard against her bulkiness in the borrowed jacket, and as his breathing became faster, so did his response to her gentle caress.

He was in charge now. *She'd* lit the fuse, but his was the explosion. He returned her kiss with a searching desperate passion that made her wilt in his arms, and as his hands unzipped the jacket, and found her slender body inside it, they seemed to melt into one being.

The kiss went on and on, its ardour increasing with each second, and Chloe knew that she wanted more. She wanted to feel her nakedness against his. She wanted fulfilment, but incredibly he was pushing her away, groaning as he did so, and at the separation of their bodies shock waves hit her.

'I must be crazy,' he panted, zipping the jacket back up again with one angry movement. 'I'm the first one to start bleating about staff members getting too friendly, especially when it's an older man and a young girl. Yet here am I, of all people, with commitments that I hold dear, doing exactly that!' He was gazing around him like a trapped animal, and with a sort of final crushing determination he announced, 'The fog's clearing. Let's go.'

Chloe was angry now. All right, *she'd* ignited the flame, but what was the matter with him? Was it because they'd been alone in the middle of nowhere, and she'd been stupid enough to issue a rash invitation that he had found too convenient to refuse?

God! She hoped *that* hadn't been his interpretation of it, but whatever he had thought it hadn't taken him long to change his mind. If there was one thing Chloe was sure of, it was that there wouldn't be another episode like it.

From now on, it would be the job and nothing else. His reaction made it seem like a sordid little office affair, and the thought of it made her feel dirty. Her job with Port Health meant a lot to her, and because she had been stupid enough to fall in love with Tom Saracen it didn't mean that she was going to do it any less efficiently.

With her back as straight as a ramrod and her head held high, she stood in the bows of the launch all the way back to the marina, and in the car for the remainder of the return journey she kept up a frozen silence.

Chloe felt his eyes on her frequently, but whatever Tom's expression, it didn't register. She couldn't bear to look at him. All she wanted was to feel the Fireblade beneath her, the wind in her face and Manchester on the approaching skyline.

'I'll drive you home,' he offered soberly. 'It will save you having to change back into the bike gear.'

She did look at him then.

'Get lost, Tom Saracen!' she hissed. 'I don't want any favours from you!' The moment they reached the house she dashed upstairs and forced her riding clothes over the top of the black dress, and with a stiff, 'Please say goodnight to your mother and Lucy for me,' she zoomed off into the night.

CHAPTER EIGHT

WHENEVER Chloe thought about Easter in the weeks that followed it was just a blur of angry misery. She had gone out with the bike club on Good Friday as arranged, but the pleasure she would normally have felt, eating up the miles along country roads, was missing. She'd had to keep reminding herself to concentrate on her driving instead of letting the moments on the fog-bound launch take over her mind.

When they had stopped for lunch Mike had asked her out again, and been a bit huffy when she'd refused.

'You look grumpy. Why?' he asked, eyeing her set face.

'I'm not grumpy,' she snapped, 'and even if I was, it's got nothing to do with you!'

He laughed, good humour returning.

'I'm not sure how to take that. Are you telling me that it has nothing to do with me because it isn't my fault that you're in a bad mood, or are you telling me to mind my own business?'

She managed a smile. 'I'm telling you that you aren't to blame.'

'Good,' he said with a mock shudder. 'I pity the guy who is. I've never seen you look so fierce before.' His face sobered. 'Because it *is* a guy, isn't it?'

'Yes, it is,' she admitted painfully, knowing that she couldn't admit to Mike that, if she let go of her anger, tears would come. . .and she would drown in them.

'So I'm not on your list of men to fancy?'

She shook her head and told him regretfully, 'I like you, Mike. You make me laugh, and you're kind.'

'But I don't make you tick?'

''Fraid not,' she told him.

Her mother had spent Easter with Edgar Harkness. They had gone to the Fylde coast, and she had come back purring, making Chloe wonder what magic the genial American had used on her petulant parent. Whatever it was, it was most welcome. Though Chloe was well aware that the outcome of the friendship might bring more loneliness for herself, there was no way she begrudged Lorraine the chance of happiness.

With regards to Tom Saracen and herself, the weeks were going by with a show of cold politeness on her part, and a quiet wariness on his, as they carried out their Port Health duties.

Chloe's absorption in the job was undiminished. Firstly, because there had been no disillusion in that area of her life, and secondly, because the harder she worked, the less the pain. It was in her free time that the misery caught up on her, when she told herself she'd behaved like an idiot for ever having imagined that an older, charismatic man like Tom would fall in love with someone so young and inexperienced as herself. Every time she thought it she told herself angrily that Chantal Mortimer was welcome to him!

There were times when she thought of asking the authorities for a transfer to another port, feeling dismally that no one would miss her. If Chloe transferred to the moon, her mother's only concern would be, was there a shop with designer labels there? As for her boss, they hadn't exchanged more than a couple of sentences in the last few weeks that weren't connected with the job.

Lucy had called into the office one day to tell her that school was great. . .and so were Maureen's boys. She had cast a cautious eye on her father through the glass that separated his office from that of his assistant, and her exuberance had dimmed somewhat when she'd whispered, 'Why don't you come to see us any more, Chloe? Have you and Dad fallen out?'

'Sort of,' she'd admitted uncomfortably.

There was no way she wanted Lucy to discover that she had made a prize fool of herself, that she had thrown herself at her father with humiliating results.

'You don't need *me* so much now, love,' Chloe said quietly. 'You've made new friends, and from the sound of it you're settling in nicely.'

'Yes, I know,' Lucy persisted, 'but Gran and I wanted to get to know you better. Just as we were all becoming friends you stopped coming.'

'I'm sorry, Lucy,' she said chokily. 'It has nothing to do with you and your gran, believe me. . .and we *are* still friends, even if we haven't seen much of each other lately. That hasn't changed. If ever I can help you in any way you have only to ask.'

'Chantal is still there every time I turn round,' Lucy wailed. 'I don't know how Dad puts up with her.'

'I thought that she seemed a nice woman when I met her,' Chloe chided gently. 'Maybe he feels that he needs someone like her.'

'*You're* what he needs!' Lucy hissed. 'Somebody young and pretty, who makes him laugh. . .and warms him up. He's off his food, and stalks around the bedroom at all hours of the night.'

Chloe had managed a weak smile.

'I can assure you that it has nothing to do with me, Lucy. The only relationship that your father wants with me is that of fellow Port Health officer. In spite of his friendship with Chantal, I feel that he still has a very poor opinion of women.'

When Lucy had gone Chloe thought dejectedly that Saracen's daughter had hit the nail on the head. She *could* warm him up, get him to white heat, even, but his thermostat had been in good working order and he had cooled down more quickly than a fire in a freezer.

Their duties over past weeks had taken them to the other end of the canal, the docks nearest to Manchester. To Partington, where a couple of tankers docked each week, and Cadishead, that could only accommodate smaller vessels carrying lube oil. Whenever they boarded ship they were careful to make sure that drinking water was pure, the crew were living under clean conditions, and there was no infestation.

One morning Tom looked up from his desk and said in clipped tones, 'We've got a company opening up in coal handling on one of the wharfs, which is a cause for gratification all round. According to the records, it's years since that was a part of the Ship Canal's function, and I'm going out there this morning to issue an Environmental Protection Act Authorisation.

'Fortunately, we in Port Health are in a position where we can stipulate conditions that they must adhere to with regard to the prevention of pollution, such as spraying the coal and wheel washing. It is such a dangerous health hazard in this day and age, and yet so often treated lightly or completely ignored.'

Chloe had listened to him with the closed expression that she adopted whenever they were together, and in return he was observing her with a keen blue gaze.

'There is no need for you to accompany me,' he said edgily, as if he'd had just about enough of her cold silences. 'You're obviously quite capable of working on your own now, and I intend to leave you to it.

'There is an Irish ship at Old Trafford dock delivering maize from Bordeaux, and we're informed that once it's unloaded it will be taking on a cargo of scrap steel for Spain. Its de-ratting certificate is due for renewal. *You* can deal with that.'

'Yes, of course,' she agreed unsmilingly, resisting an angry urge to touch her forelock and bow. She was so aware of him that she felt faint. Tom Saracen was even more desirable now that he was completely out of reach.

'Do you want a lift, as we're both going in the same direction?' he asked tonelessly.

'No, thanks. I'll use the bike.'

'Just as you like.' He was picking up the case that held his papers and other Port Health equipment, and said with a smile that didn't reach his eyes, 'I'll stand you lunch on Salford Quays if you want to catch up with me later.'

Chloe stared at him. Was he suggesting a truce? She didn't think so. After weeks of non-involvement, and being told only seconds ago that he wasn't panting for her company, he was extending a lame invitation to join him for a meal. So what was at the back of it?

'Thanks just the same, but I've brought a sandwich,' she said flatly.

It was a lie. He wasn't the only one who wasn't sleeping. After a wakeful night she had dropped off to sleep in the dawn, and got up with barely time to shower and get dressed before it was time to get the Fireblade out. As for making a sandwich, there had been no chance, but she'd had to find some excuse for not eating with him.

'Maybe you'd be prepared to give it a miss, and agree to my suggestion, as there is something I'd like to discuss with you,' he said with stilted politeness.

'About the job?' she asked quickly.

'No, not about the job.'

Chloe's heart began to hammer. What, then? What could he possibly have to discuss that wasn't about Port Health? Maybe *he* was going to suggest she get a transfer. . .so that he could replace her with one of his own sex. He'd be happier that way, no doubt, and she thought that the long-dead Herta was reaching out with watery fingers to complicate *her* life as well as his.

'Yes, all right, then,' she agreed reluctantly as he prepared to leave. 'I'll see you at Salford Quays.'

He had only been gone a matter of minutes when port control came through to say that the captain of a ship about to dock at Eastham was reporting an animal on board.

Chloe thought quickly. The ship at Old Trafford docks wasn't due to leave immediately, whereas it was important that the vessel with the animal on board was made aware of the rabies regulations before any infringement occurred. That being so, it would have to be her first call.

The captain was English, an elderly man with a grey beard and sharp hazel eyes. When she put in an appearance he said, 'I've got my cat on board. . .a ginger tom. He was here a minute ago.' He looked around him and called, 'Here, Neptune! Here, my beauty!'

'I see that you've come from a foreign port,' she said sternly, 'and I'm sure you are aware that the cat should have been locked up from the moment of entering the docks. It will have to be kept in that situation until your ship leaves. In the meantime, I must ask you to read this notice regarding the prevention of rabies, and sign it, and perhaps while you're doing that you can instruct the crew to find the missing cat.'

The captain did as he was asked on all counts, but the cat didn't appear, and Chloe warned him, 'I'll give you until after lunch to produce it, Captain. If it isn't found by the time I come back I shall conclude it has escaped ashore, and you will be prosecuted.'

'It'll be here,' he promised quickly. 'Neptune don't stray far.'

'He's strayed far enough by the looks of it,' she said warningly. 'I hope that for your sake you can produce the animal when I come back.'

During her inspection of the ship on Old Trafford dock Chloe discovered that there had been some problem with the drinking water. It appeared that a pipeline carrying non-potable liquid had been wrongly sited during repairs, and it had contaminated the water supply. The piping had since been re-routed, but it left the problem of decontaminating the drinking-water tank.

While the ship was in dock the problem wasn't urgent as there was fresh water to hand all the time, but once it was time for it to set sail the tank would have to be ready to be refilled with potable water. She instructed the crew to disinfect it with a chlorine solution of 50mg per litre of water for twenty-four hours. The heavily chlorinated water must then be emptied and the system flushed with potable water before refilling with a supply that would be drunk by the crew.

There were no other problems on board and she issued a renewal of the certificate without any further preamble, and then made her way to the unexpected rendezvous with Tom Saracen.

He was waiting for her beside one of the floating restaurants on the elegant waterside development that had replaced the derelict Salford docks. They had once been one of the United Kingdom's busiest ports until the seventies, when changes in trade patterns and the introduction of containers had made them commercially unsound. In 1982 the docks had been closed and shipping had no longer pursued its way along the Ship Canal to the upper reaches.

Brilliant planning and design had brought Salford Quays out of the waste dockland, and now huge commercial enterprises had moved their offices out there, and a smart residential area had been established overlooking the quays.

Today there was colour and activity everywhere as the office staff from the business complexes came out into the sun to eat their lunches on the terraces and in the gardens beside the water, and the man she had come to meet stood out among them.

Tall, unsmiling, the sun glinting on the dark gloss of his hair and on the gold strips on his shoulders, he made all the other men appear commonplace. In spite of her intention to keep her feelings under tight control, it didn't stop her heart from missing a beat.

This was a place dear to Chloe's heart. She had watched the transformation with delight, and had tried to persuade her mother to buy an apartment on the Quays instead of in the centre of Manchester, but Lorraine wouldn't hear of it. Anything connected with the canal was not her scene.

'We'll eat first and talk afterwards, if that's all right with you,' Tom said when she reached his side.

Chloe wasn't going to argue. Her cool new image didn't allow for that, but her appetite wasn't going to be at its best with the thought of what might be coming after!

'Fine by me,' she agreed, and he led the way on to the bottom deck of the restaurant.

Thomas looked around him, keen eyes noting the bar arrangement and the dining facilities, and he said, 'I shouldn't imagine Port Health have much trouble with this place. How often is it inspected?'

'According to your predecessor, rarely,' she told him, 'as it meets with all the criteria for the serving and preparation of food.'

'How was your morning?' he asked as they waited for their meals to be brought to them.

'Interesting,' she told him briefly, and went on to describe the episodes of the missing cat and the contaminated water.

'You've obviously dealt with both matters satisfactorily,' he said with a wintry smile. 'I'll come with you

when you go back to check on the missing animal, but
I haven't asked you here for us to spend our lunch-
hour talking about the job.'

He was toying with the stem of his glass, twisting it
round in strong brown fingers, and she found herself
watching him hypnotically. She was itching to know
why he had asked her here, yet on the other hand she
wasn't sure that she would be able to cope with
whatever he was going to say. If it was something
unpleasant, she hoped that she would have the presence of mind to face up to it without giving herself
away.

When they had finished eating Tom said, 'Shall we
have a stroll in the sunshine for a few minutes?'

'Yes, if you like,' she agreed reluctantly.

There were less people around now—the lunch-hour
was over for most of them—and they had the walkway
on Salford Wharf, which had been created as part of
the Ship Canal's and the docks' centenary, to
themselves.

A couple at the other side of the harbour stopped
and clasped their arms around each other, kissing
lingeringly as they did so. As they watched them Chloe
said impulsively, '*He* doesn't seem to have any
inhibitions.'

She didn't need to explain the remark. His face
tightened and he said with gravelly perception, 'Maybe
he isn't a widower with a teenage daughter, an elderly
mother. . .and an assistant who behaves on a level
with his daughter.'

'Meaning?' she asked angrily.

'This is hardly the moment for us to start arguing,'

he sidetracked, 'seeing that I have a favour to ask of you.'

This was a turn-up for the book!

'What is it?' she asked carefully. As she remembered Lucy's pessimistic warnings there came to mind a distorted image of herself walking down the aisle behind Thomas and Chantal.

'My mother is going on an extended visit to her sisters in Australia on Saturday,' he said as his direct gaze met her puzzled eyes.

'Yes?' she questioned.

'And I don't want anything to prevent her from going.'

'Of course,' she murmured, still confused. 'So what's the problem?'

'The problem is that I have to go into hospital for a few days next week for some tests, which will leave Lucy on her own. If my mother gets to hear of it she will cancel the holiday and I don't want her to do that. I wondered if *you* would mind staying with Lucy?'

Anguished concern wiped out her anger in a split-second. If anything happened to him she would go into holy orders! But instead of reassuring him with regard to his daughter, Chloe found herself saying, 'Wouldn't you rather she stayed with Chantal?'

He smiled, and there was a sudden weariness in it. 'If you mean, would that be more convenient for everyone. . .yes, but Lucy doesn't like Chantal. She thinks she's going to be having her as a stepmother.'

'And is she?' she asked carefully.

Thomas shook his head. 'I'm not planning anything at the moment, other than getting this hospital business sorted out.'

'Of course I'll look after Lucy,' she said with quick contrition. 'But what's wrong? Why do you need the tests?'

'It's nothing for *you* to worry about,' he said dismissively, and glanced at his watch as if the discussion was over.

Chloe turned her head away. What was that supposed to mean? That she was welcome in the guise of companion for Lucy during his absence, but that there was no other role for her to play in his life? Or was he merely trying to reassure her? One thing was for certain—he hadn't been prepared to enlighten her as to why he was going to be hospitalised.

When they got back to the scene of the missing cat they parked their respective vehicles further along the dockside and proceeded towards the ship in question. She wasn't expecting any problems, having made it clear to the captain that he would be in big trouble if his animal hadn't been found and put in a secure place by the time she returned.

It was a small ship with a small crew, and none of them was in sight as they stood looking up at it. As Tom prepared to go on board he stopped in mid-stride and she looked at him questioningly.

He pointed to both the right and left of them, and her eyes widened. The captain, red-faced and perspiring, was hurrying along the dockside from one direction with a ginger tom cat under his arm, and the mate was approaching from the other, carrying an animal of similar origin. As the two Port Health officers eyed them in amazement, Tom began to laugh. At the top of the companionway that led on to the ship was the missing culprit, contentedly licking its paws.

'There's our missing cat,' he grinned. 'It must have come out of hiding while those two guys were looking for a replacement.' As the two seamen stood by in embarrassed silence she joined him in laughter.

It must have been panic stations, Chloe thought, when they couldn't find the cat, and with the prospect of a heavy fine staring them in the face they had gone to search for a replica, only to end up with two, the original contentedly awaiting their return!

'Oh, what a tangled web we weave, eh, Captain!' Tom said when he'd instructed them to secure the truant cat immediately, and return the two look-alikes to where they had found them.

On the way back to the office they laughed uproariously, and with the combination of their shared amusement, and his asking her for help with regard to Lucy, the atmosphere was warmer than it had been in weeks.

Yet it didn't really alter anything, Chloe told herself as she went into the empty apartment that night. Tom Saracen had asked for her help, and she was only too happy to give it, but it appeared that it was the only way he *did* need her. He didn't require her to fall in his arms, or warm his bed, and so she would have to be content with what was on offer.

When she went into work after the weekend, Tom informed her that his mother had flown out to Australia as arranged, and that her own presence would be required as from Tuesday evening.

'I'm going into hospital in the morning,' he said, 'and so, if you could go to our place right after you've finished here, Lucy will be waiting. I'm not sure how long they'll keep me in, but rest assured, the moment I'm out you'll be off the hook.'

That was what *he* thought, she observed glumly. She had been hooked ever since that first day when she had looked up from the sample of nuts on the quayside to find him standing beside her, and nothing had changed. It was just unfortunate that she had fallen in love with a man who saw her as an older version of his daughter, and who wasn't too keen on women in any case.

Ever since he had mentioned the hospital appointment she had found herself scrutinising him for signs of illness, but without success. He showed no signs of pain or fatigue, and looked his normal healthy self, but she wasn't so foolish that she didn't know that people could look healthy when they were dying. Maybe if Thomas wasn't prepared to enlighten her. . . Lucy would.

It was busy on the port without him during Tuesday, and as she was leaving in the late afternoon Chloe saw that a big Dutch ship carrying lube oil was heading for Stanlow. She made a mental note of it and decided that if her presence was required on board for any reason it would have to wait until tomorrow, as she didn't want Lucy coming home from school to an empty house.

She'd had to do it for almost all her life and was used to it, but as far as Lucy was concerned a couple of days ago there had been three of them, and tonight she was alone.

Lucy seemed happy enough when Chloe caught up with her on the way home, and it was obvious that it

was partly due to having *her* company while her father
was away.

They prepared the meal together, laughing and
chatting as they did so, and when there was a lull in
the conversation Chloe asked casually, 'What is wrong
with your dad, Lucy?'

'I'm not sure,' she said vaguely, 'except that it's
something to do with his bone marrow.'

Chloe found herself gripping the edge of the sink
unit as the dreaded implications of what Lucy had said
appeared   ghoul-like   in   her   mind—leukaemia,
Hodgkin's disease, severe aplastic anaemia, to name
but a few!

She sank down on to the nearest chair, and Lucy,
showing the first signs of anxiety, said, 'It's not serious,
is it?'

'I shouldn't think so,' Chloe told her, rallying
because she didn't want to frighten the child. There
was no point in alarming Lucy until there was cause
for it, she reasoned. Although the mere thought of the
dark prince of the canal having that sort of problem to
face was horrendous, Chloe knew he would take a dim
view of his daughter being distressed on his account.

'I'll take you to visit him after we've eaten,' she
offered, but Lucy shook her head.

'Dad left strict instructions this morning that he
doesn't want any visitors. He said that he'd prefer me
to get on with my homework.'

And what had he said about herself she wondered. . .'Don't let that young nymphomaniac from
the office get near me'?

His bedroom had been made available for her once
more, but she couldn't sleep. She was imagining him

locked away in a plastic bubble for weeks on end in a desperate effort to save his life, and she wept for the sadness of it all.

The following day Chloe had no time to dwell on her anxiety over Tom. She had no sooner set foot inside Port House than the Department of Transport were on the line requesting her to attend a joint inspection, along with themselves and a pest-control company, of a Nigerian ship that had docked late the previous night. It had been arrested by them on arrival after signs of rodent droppings had been observed.

Aware that this could be the rarity that Tom had warned her about, she made her way to the dock with all speed. As she joined the two men already on board she was amazed to discover that the vessel had over sixty crew members, which by present-day standards amounted to gross overmanning.

As they proceeded to inspect it she was appalled by the conditions prevailing. There were huge cock-roaches everywhere. The galley was filthy, with accumulated grease and food debris on all sides. Bread dough was rising among the insects, the fridge was out of order, and the freezer filthy.

In a cupboard in one of the passages rodent drop-pings had been found, and the greasy runs that Chloe had been trained to look out for which came from the fur of the rodents, because of their fondness for oily conditions, were visible on the lagging in the cupboard.

With each step she took in the company of the Department of Transport representative and the pest-control expert Chloe's amazement increased. Due to the excess of crew, the men were packed four to a cabin, which was bad enough, but on top of that, every conceivable inch of space was crammed with electrical goods in various stages of repair.

Seeing her disbelief, one of her companions commented, 'They've got a nice little sideline going on here. This lot will net them a small fortune when they get back to Nigeria.'

She nodded grimly. 'Maybe, but they won't be going anywhere until they've done some drastic sanitorising of the ship.'

Surprisingly, water samples taken from several points on board had proved to be satisfactory, due entirely to the fact that fresh supplies had been taken on in recent days while anchored at the Mersey Bar.

The duty of Port Health with regard to the situation was clear enough, and Chloe knew that she must serve notices on both the captain and the shipping agents. One in respect of rodent disinfestation, and a second referring to a similar procedure with the insects.

Although there had been evidence of rats, both she and the pest-control expert were puzzled, as the signs found were too small for a rat, and too large for a mouse. When she got back to the office she reached out a file regarding rodents in West Africa, and in it were details of a small rat indigenous to Nigeria called the Coucha rat.

It had been known to carry the plague and Lassa fever, and Chloe knew immediately that the other organisations that she had been with on the ship must be informed of the public-health risk.

The insanitory conditions would require three disinfestation treatments to bring the ship back up to a standard where it was no longer a health risk, and they would be left to the pest-control people. In the meantime, any current de-ratting certificate was invalid, and would continue to be so until the vessel was in a much improved condition.

It wouldn't be allowed to leave the port until all conditions stipulated by Port Health, in the guise of herself, had been complied with. Hopefully by then Tom Saracen would be back holding the reins. She was satisfied with the way she had done her part in preventing what could have been a major health hazard, to not only the ship's crew, but also people on the mainland. She wouldn't be easy in her mind until she had his approval.

At the thought of him, the anxiety came back, and Maureen, eyeing Chloe's worried face, suggested, 'It's only an hour to home time—why don't you get off now? You've had a taxing day, and I'm sure that our chief port health officer would have been proud of his little fledgling if he'd seen how you've coped.'

Chloe managed a tired smile. 'I wonder?'

'Any news from the hospital?' she asked of Lucy the moment she got in.

'I've only just got in myself,' she said, 'and haven't had time to see if there are any messages.'

There wasn't. No crisp voice coming over the answering machine to give a bulletin on his progress, or to demand a report on how they were coping, and Chloe wondered how he could go away and cut himself off from them like that. Maybe it was Tom Saracen's way of facing up to the scourge that might be threatening him, she thought in silent anguish, or perhaps for once he was putting himself first.

She could find out, of course, by phoning the hospital

or visiting him, but he had specifically said they were not to visit, and that was something else she didn't understand. Visitors were often the only pleasant part of the day for the hospital patient.

A frightening thought struck her. Was what they were going to do to him so awful that he didn't want to be observed? Lucy didn't seem to see anything sinister in the fact that he hadn't been in touch, and when she saw Chloe's fraught expression she said calmly, 'Dad knows what he's doing, Chloe. He will either just turn up, or get in touch when he's ready. He wouldn't have told us not to visit if there'd been anything to panic about.'

Chloe eyed her fondly. Saracen's daughter had the same logical mind as her father. . .and Lucy had known him a lot longer than herself. But she was still only a child, and there was no way he would want her upset, even if he was dying.

Chloe pulled herself together and said with a strained smile, 'I'm sure that you're right, but I don't see the harm in a phone call. . .to the ward sister, for example.'

'Are you a relative?' a guarded voice asked at the other end of the line when she was put through.

'Er—no, I'm afraid not, but I am in charge of Mr Saracen's young daughter,' Chloe said persuasively.

'I see,' the voice replied. 'In that case, I can tell you that he has had the necessary removal and is recovering well. We will let you know when he is due to be discharged.'

Removal! Removal of what? she wondered, but because of the instructions he had left, for the life of her she couldn't ask.

'So he's all right?' she persisted.

'Yes, he's fine. Just a little drowsy from the anaesthetic.'

'How is he?' Lucy asked when she went back into the sitting-room.

'Everything seems to be satisfactory, according to the ward sister,' she said with a reassuring smile. 'They will give us a buzz when he's ready to come home. I wonder if he'll be able to drive?'

'Yes, of course he will,' Lucy said confidently. 'He said it wasn't anything serious.'

'That's all right, then,' Chloe murmured, with the words 'bone marrow' hammering away inside her head.

When they had eaten and washed up, she looked at the clock. It was going to be a long night. Lucy had gone upstairs to do some homework, and Chloe looked around for something to occupy herself with. She *had* to get Tom out of her mind, close it to the awful possibilities that she kept dredging up, and she decided that once she had showered and changed out of her uniform she would find a good book.

She had one foot on the first step of the stairs when the bell rang, and she paused. Who could it be? Chantal, perhaps, enquiring about Tom, or a double-glazing salesman? She straightened up. There was only one way to find out.

A man was standing in the porch, burly, blue-eyed and with the same Nordic colouring as herself. As she eyed him questioningly he said in slow surprise, 'I am Peter Hagenbaach. . .and you. . .are. . .from the port? Yes?'

He was eyeing her uniform and she said warily, 'Yes. I am. What's the problem?'

He smiled behind a beard of the same colour as his hair. 'There is no problem. I am here to see my brother-in-law and my niece.'

Before Chloe had time to digest that surprising statement Lucy's voice squeaked excitedly at her elbow, 'Uncle Peter!'

CHAPTER NINE

THE evening that had promised to drag flew as they entertained Lucy's Dutch uncle. Herta's brother, for indeed it was he, was amusing, attractive, and when *his* blue eyes focused on her Chloe found them a lot warmer than his brother-in-law's had been in recent weeks.

Any awkwardness at meeting a stranger in such circumstances had been banished when she discovered that he was the master of the big tanker that she had seen heading for Stanlow when she'd been biking to the house the previous night. She told the smiling Dutchman, 'Tom told me that he was acquainted with someone who had a very smart vessel, and he promised to take me on board. Obviously he must have been referring to you.'

'But, of course, you must come aboard. You will be most welcome, Chloe,' he told her in his excellent English, 'but what about Thomas? It is most unfortunate that he is ill. I will visit him, if it is permitted.'

'It's permitted by the hospital,' Lucy chipped in, 'but not by Dad. It isn't anything serious, Uncle Peter. He'll soon be home. That's why he isn't bothered about visitors.'

When their visitor looked across at her for confirmation Chloe shrugged awkwardly. She wasn't going to tell him that she was worried sick about Tom, or Peter Hagenbaach would be concerned too, and curious as well, as to why Tom Saracen's assistant was so involved in his affairs. He wouldn't see anything strange in her chaperoning Lucy, but if he discovered how much Tom was in her thoughts it *would* be cause for conjecture.

'Thomas is a very lucky man to have such a charming young officer under his command,' he said as he was taking his leave at close on midnight. He took her hand and looked down on the ringless fingers. 'And one who is not married, too,' he finished softly.

There were various replies she could have made to his comments, such as, it hadn't taken him long to make a pass at her, or that she'd left her wedding-ring at home, or that she was just as committed to someone as if she *were* married, but that she was the only one who knew anything about it.

'Come and dine on my ship tomorrow,' he coaxed. 'You can always come again with Tom when he is better, but tomorrow I will show you around one of Rotterdam's finest ships.'

After a day spent with rat droppings and cockroaches, it was a tempting offer, to be fussed over for once. Why shouldn't she accept the invitation? The Dutchman might be a charmer, but what was wrong with that? Charm had been in short supply in her life of late.

'Yes, all right, I will,' she told him. 'Subject to my not being called away to another part of the port.'

'Make sure that you are not,' he said persuasively.

She could only tell him smilingly, 'I'll try.'

Compared to the other vessels she had been on, the Dutch ship was palatial and all aspects of the accom-

modation were first class. As Peter Hagenbaach had
shown her around, Chloe's face had become more
sober by the minute. As he escorted her into a smart
dining area where a table was laid for two, he asked,
'What is it, Chloe? Do you not like my ship?'

She smiled. 'Of course I do. It's fantastic. I was just
thinking about the crew of a Nigerian ship I was on
yesterday, and will be visiting again shortly. The poor
men were packed on board like sardines, in absolute
squalor, having to do electrical repairs on an assort-
ment of second-hand goods into the bargain.' She
grimaced at the thought. 'It was awful!'

'That is because they are not organised,' he said
briefly. 'Nothing is achieved without organisation. My
company is very prosperous because I work hard, and
think hard. But come, let us forget about them and
eat. . .drink. . .and get acquainted.'

The food was delicious, the wine excellent, and her
host entertaining company. He had come round the
table to fill her glass, and with his arm around her
shoulders she was laughing up at him with the empty
glass in her hand when a voice spoke from the doorway
behind her.

'What have we here, then?' Tom Saracen asked with
quiet irony. 'While the chief's away. . .Port Health
will play?'

Chloe swivelled slowly to face him; her heart was
leaping with relief and pleasure, and yet why did he
always have to make her feel at a disadvantage? 'Port
Health will play,' he'd said. She hadn't been doing
much playing while he had been away. She hadn't had
a minute to call her own, and yet the second she did
relax, he was there, eyeing her as if she was the

original drone. But she mustn't go on griping about
that. Thankfully, whatever ailed him, he was back. . .
on two feet. . .and moving towards his brother-in-law.

'Peter!' he said warmly. 'Good to see you.'

'How are you, Thomas?' the Dutchman said.

'Fine,' Tom said easily.

Chloe felt tears sting her eyelids. Why was he always
so low-key about everything? So withdrawn and self-
sufficient? Her eyes were raking his face for signs of
anything different, but he looked just the same as
always, a bit tired perhaps, fine drawn, but wasn't that
how he always looked?

'I'll get my man to lay an extra place,' Peter
Hagenbaach was saying, but Tom shook his head.

'No, thanks just the same, Peter. I had an early
lunch before I left the hospital. I came to find Chloe,
to let her know I'm home, and that she can relax now.'

That was a laugh, she thought. She wasn't going to
relax until she knew what was wrong with him, but it
was hardly the time to start questioning him, and so
she said, 'How did you know I was here?'

'Maureen told me. I called in at the office and she
said you were dining out.'

'Yes,' Peter interrupted. 'I called round at the house
last night. Of course, you weren't there, but I was
entertained by Chloe and young Lucy. Your delightful
assistant told me that you had said you would bring
her on board when next I docked, and so I invited her
to have lunch with me on the spot.' He laughed. 'We
were getting on famously and now you've come and
spoiled it.'

Chloe felt her face start to burn. That was laying it
on a bit thick. They had merely been having a meal

and a few laughs, but he was making it sound as if they had been ready to jump into bed. It looked as if Tom Saracen thought the same as he said levelly, 'Yes, well, I'm sorry to break it up, but I do have to get up to date on my domestic situation, and what has been happening with regard to the job while I've been away, so if you've finished, Chloe, perhaps Peter will excuse us? You must come up to the house for a meal before you sail,' he told the Dutchman on a warmer note.

'I shall be delighted,' he said without hesitation. 'Just as long as Chloe will be there.'

'Chloe?' Tom echoed, as if he had never heard the name before. 'Yes, well, we'll have to see.' As she got to her feet he said, 'Bye for now, Peter.'

The moment they were alone Chloe said uncomfortably, 'Your brother-in-law's invitation was so pressing I couldn't very well refuse.'

'No, I'm sure you couldn't,' he said drily. 'It was quite clear you were enjoying yourself immensely. Perhaps I should warn you that Peter has a woman in every port. The conquest of the fair sex comes easy to him.'

'How dare you insinuate that I was up to no good there?' she flared. 'And if your brother-in-law is popular with the women I'm not surprised, as he is absolutely charming. I accepted his invitation because he was a relative of yours, and not for any other reason. You might have caught me laughing, but I can assure you that it's the first time in days that I've felt like it.'

'Why is that?'

Tears were threatening as she tried to grapple with his insensitivity, and there was a break in her voice as she said, 'Why? You ask why? Because I've been out of my mind with worry!'

'What about?'

'You really do like to turn the knife, don't you?' she cried. 'Lucy said you had something wrong with your bone marrow, and I've been. . .'

Chloe couldn't go on any longer. She turned her head away and wept. He didn't speak, didn't attempt to touch her, there was just silence, and then he gave a groaning sort of sigh.

'You thought I was ill?' he breathed.

'What was I supposed to think?' she cried through the tears.

'Come here,' he said, and when she stepped towards him he drew her to him and patted the top of her head. 'Did I or did I not tell you that there was nothing for you to worry about?'

'Yes, you did,' she gulped, 'but nobody goes for tests on their bone marrow if there is no cause for alarm.'

'I went in to *donate* my bone marrow,' he said patiently. 'I'm on the register, and they needed it for someone who *is* very ill. So, you see, there *was* no cause for alarm. If you want to hear the details, the bone marrow was drawn from my breast bone to be transplanted into the patient. Does that satisfy you?'

'No, it doesn't,' she flung at him, rage engulfing her now that she knew she'd worried for nothing. 'I had you with all sorts of horrendous diseases! Why did it have to be such a big secret? Why couldn't you have said why you were going into hospital?'

He laughed, and she could have hit him. 'Because

I'm not used to being fussed over, and I didn't think anyone would be interested.'

Her anger was fading, leaving behind it a deadly calm as she told him, 'If ever the day dawns when you can admit that you need someone else, that you're not totally self-sufficient, I might be around, but don't bank on it, not while there are men like Peter Hagenbaach and my friend Mike happy to have my company.'

There were clothes and toiletries belonging to her at Tom's house, but there was no way she was going for them. . .not today. After those brief fraught moments on the dockside beside the Dutch ship she needed time to gather her wits.

Tom had gone back home, informing her curtly that he would be back on the job in the morning, and as far as she was concerned that was soon enough to have to face him again. The things she had left at his house could stay there until he either brought them to the office, or she felt calm enough to go for them.

As she had driven back to Port House it was with the dismal knowledge that she'd given herself away again, let him see how much she cared, and in return he had given her a fatherly pat on the head, and humoured her with the basic details of what had been done to him in hospital.

Peter Hagenbaach radioed in, late in the afternoon, expressing his regret that her visit to his ship had been cut short.

'It *was* only supposed to be my lunch-break,' she reminded him.

'Yes, I know that,' he agreed, 'but I did detect an

urgency on the part of Thomas to get you out of my clutches.'

'Maybe, she countered, 'but I assure you that it was only for practical reasons.'

'I think not. I have not seen that expression on his face in many long years, since before my sister died. She was very like you in appearance, you know. She had the same golden fairness, the slender body and the pleasant face.'

'Yes. Lucy told me that her mother had hair the same colour as mine, but I'd imagined her to be more. . .' She hesitated. More what? More like a female Viking?

'More wilful and selfish than yourself, were you going to say? Because if you were, it is the truth. Herta cared only for herself, her ship, and Thomas, in that order.'

'And Lucy?' she questioned.

'Ah, yes. The little Lucy was not part of her plans. She was an unexpected encumbrance.'

Chloe's throat tightened. Lucy of the dark hair and eyes, whom she had only known for a short time, and yet was already so fond of, had been seen as an encumbrance by her mother. Who better than herself to understand the pain of that?

Hadn't Lorraine shown *her* often enough that she was in the way? Fortunately for Lucy she'd had a father who had made up for it, who had given up the sea to be with her. Chloe thought wistfully that, considering the pattern his life had taken, he couldn't be blamed for relying on no one but himself.

'And so you will come again?' the Dutchman was saying.

'Given the opportunity. . .yes,' she agreed, and knew that she wouldn't be pushing it, even though he was an attractive and interesting man.

'And what do we have here?' Thomas asked the next morning as he eyed the paperwork on his desk.

Chloe had written out a preliminary report on her visit to the Nigerian ship for his enlightenment, and it was on top of the pile. There would have to be a much more detailed report presented by Port Health when the ship had been brought up to standard, but in the meantime she had listed the basic problems.

There was new tiling to be done in the kitchen and toilet areas, and fridge repairs, which was incredible when the ship's crew were engaged in mending electrical goods. New catering equipment was required among a host of other things, the biggest and most important of which was the massive disinfestation programme that was already under way.

Another visit by Port Health would be required very soon to make sure that all the improvements were being done. Whether it would be made by herself, or her boss, Chloe didn't know. She wasn't bothered either way, just as long as he didn't suggest they did it together.

She had been the first to arrive, with Maureen some minutes later, Thomas almost on her heels. Chloe and he had exchanged a cool 'good morning', and when Maureen had asked him how he was after his stay in hospital Chloe had gone downstairs into the computer-room to avoid taking part in the conversation. It was when she had gone back up that she had found him scrutinising the report.

'So! We have a problem on our hands,' he said.

'Yes, a big one,' she affirmed. 'I've never seen anything like it in my life!'

'Mmm. These things do happen, but they're few and far between in this day and age, thank God!'

He looked up at her then, the incredible blue eyes meeting her own blank stare, and said, 'I'm sorry I caused you anxiety, Chloe. It never occurred to me that you might be worried. I felt I was inconveniencing you enough by asking you to stay with Luce, and was intent on not adding to it with *my* affairs. The next time I go into hospital I'll see that you're fully briefed before I'm admitted.'

If that was sarcasm, he could get lost, she thought stonily. He wasn't going to get under her skin today. Oh, dear, no! She had done enough agonising over him during the past few days to last a lifetime, and so she said coolly, 'Why? Is that likely?'

'No, of course not, unless I fall into one of the locks, or get crushed between two ships, or split my head open on an overhanging pipe, all of which are catastrophes that have happened to past and present Port Health officers,' he told her with a quizzical smile.

'*I'm* more likely to do that than you,' she said, not to be thawed. 'You are too well-organised.'

A shadow crossed his face. 'You think so?'

'Well, aren't you?'

'Yes, in some ways.' There was an ironic twist to his mouth, and he changed the subject. He pointed to the report.

'You dealt with this admirably, Chloe. I'm proud of you.'

'Thanks,' she said casually, without meeting his

eyes, and was given the chance to escape by the phone ringing in her office.

It was her mother, calling from America. She had been there a month as the guest of Edgar Harkness, and was showing no inclination to come home.

'Chloe?' she said.

'Yes, Mother?'

'I have news for you.'

Chloe straightened up in her chair. 'Oh, yes? What is it?'

'I'm getting married in two weeks' time, here in New York. I am expecting you to be there.'

'Why? I thought you didn't like folks knowing you had a twenty-eight-year-old daughter,' Chloe said perversely.

It would have been so much nicer if her mother had said 'Do please be there for me', or 'I do hope you will be able to get leave from your job and come', but no, Lorraine was running true to form. Because Chloe was feeling thoroughly out of sorts, she didn't feel like making it easy for her.

There was a moment of surprised silence and then her mother surfaced again. 'Edgar has *three* daughters,' she said stiffly, 'so there is no problem.'

Chloe began to laugh, but there was no mirth in it. So she didn't have to be a skeleton in the closet with regard to the bridegroom's family—that was the first big joke, and the second was, how would her mother cope with all that competition?

'Yes, all right, I'll be there,' she promised on a more sober note. 'What are you going to do about the apartment? Are you coming back to sort out your affairs?'

'No,' Lorraine said decisively. 'Sell the apartment. Keep half the money, and send me the remainder when it's all settled. I will be living in downtown Manhattan most of the time,' she said, her voice lifting. 'Not far from 42nd Street. Isn't that marvellous?'

'Yes, marvellous,' Chloe agreed flatly.

When her mother had gone off the line, she leaned back in the swivel chair behind her desk and gazed blankly into space. As the minutes went by she started to face up to the future. She really would be on her own now. Although there hadn't been much communication between her mother and herself, at least they'd had each other; now Lorraine was getting herself a wealthy husband and Chloe was being left to do the best she could, but, she decided, it wasn't all gloom.

She would be able to buy herself a small cottage with her share of the money from the sale of the apartment, and if there was one to be had it would be at Pickering's Lock on the Weaver. It was a remote and beautiful spot. In days gone by, when the area was known for its salt, pack horses would bring it down to the lock to be loaded on to small boats that sailed to Liverpool on the tide, and even now, because of its isolation, the children from the cottages there had to sail across the river to get to school. Second only to Tom Saracen's house overlooking the Ship Canal, it was the place where she would most like to live.

'What's wrong?' his voice asked from the doorway. 'You look—er—strange.'

'I feel it,' she said woodenly. 'That was my mother on the phone from New York. She's getting married in a few weeks' time, and demands my presence.'

His face darkened. 'Just like that?'

'Just like that,' she echoed.

'Had you any idea?'

'I thought it might be on the cards, though certainly not with such speed. I suppose if my mother has got her grappling irons into a rich fish, she isn't going to let him get away, to put it in nautical terms, which seems to be the only way I think these days.'

'Oh? And what does that mean?'

She managed a smile. 'I see Lucy as a pretty young mermaid, your brother-in-law as King Neptune, and yourself as a rock.'

'Yes, I thought I might be something boring,' he said wryly. 'And what about yourself?'

'A shipwreck?' she said succinctly, and his eyebrows lifted.

'I'd say more of a trim little craft, but why all the moralising? Is it because your mother is getting married?'

'Not exactly,' she told him tightly. 'It's because I can't seem to keep afloat these days.'

'There's nothing wrong with the way you're doing the job,' he said decisively, and she wondered if he was being deliberately obtuse.

'I'm not talking about the job,' she told him with a bright spot of colour on each cheek, but he wasn't to be drawn. His mind was still on her news from America.

'I presume that your mother intends to live over there?' he questioned.

'Yes, in Manhattan.'

'Well, at least you'll have the apartment.'

''Fraid not,' she told him prosaically.

'How do you mean?' he asked, his mouth a tight slit of disapproval.

'My mother has just instructed me to sell it. I am to be allowed to keep half of the proceeds, and she wants the rest.'

'And she's marrying a rich American! You don't deserve to be treated this way,' he said angrily.

'I don't deserve a lot of things, but they seem to come my way, nevertheless,' she said with a sigh.

He ignored the dig, and said, the anger still in him, 'So what are you going to do?'

'Buy a cottage somewhere near Pickering's Lock, and do my own thing.'

'And what might that be?'

'Put the "urban street tiger" to good use, and buy a rowing boat to get me across the river.'

'And that's it?'

'Why? What else did you expect?'

'I really don't know,' he said warily.

'Oh, I forgot to mention—I'll be accepting any invitations that come my way from handsome Dutch captains and suchlike,' she told him with innocent mockery. 'At least *he* doesn't blame all my sex for the shortcomings of one of them.'

He reached forward and grabbed her wrists, bringing her to her feet in one movement. When their eyes were only inches apart he flared, 'Neither do I! I don't blame anybody for anything, Chloe. Can we get that clear? But just as I don't blame them, neither do I want sympathy or charity from them either, and that includes you! You're young, and fresh, and lovely, and an ever-present thorn in my side, but I've built a protective armour around me over the years, and damn me, if I don't find a chink in it every time you turn on the charm.'

'Turn on the charm!' she shrieked. 'What do you think I am? Some kind of evil Lorelei out to wreck your life again?'

He was eyeing her as if hypnotised. As his arms came around her like bands of steel, and his lips parted, ready to claim hers, he murmured, 'The rock has just turned into molten lava!'

Maureen's footsteps on the stairs outside forced them to separate, and by the time she came into the office area they were standing a foot apart, eyes locked, the heat of their encounter like a tangible thing in the air, and then he turned and went back into his office.

'Whoops!' Maureen said. 'Have I interrupted something?'

Chloe nodded. 'Yes, you've just prevented me from making a fool of myself for the umpteenth time.'

They visited the Nigerian ship again the next day. . . together.

'This is *your* operation,' Tom said when they discussed it in the morning. 'You were in at the beginning, and I want you to see it through, but I'm going to come and have a look for myself, and I think that this morning is as good a time as any.'

It was the same between them as before—no sooner was she in his arms than she was out of them, and they were back to a polite working relationship. But she could cope with that. It was the other thing that haunted her nights and bedevilled her days, her love for a man who wasn't used to indulging himself, who was honourable in his commitment to his family, and wary of change.

He had explained. He had been bitten once, and it had been a large bite, so big that he thought that every woman he met had shark's teeth. Tom Saracen hadn't had to watch his wife's affection go to another man. His rival had been on a much bigger scale. He had fought the waters that joined lands together in cruel magnificence.

But what about Chantal? According to Lucy, he didn't put up the barricades when she was around, and that must mean one of two things: either she had got through his defences, or she meant so little to him that he saw no cause to keep her at arm's length. Whatever the reason, Chloe would very much like to know.

The first of the disinfestation treatments had been done when they got there, with Permethrin dusting powder, Bromard baits, and various other substances. The galley deck had been retiled, and the cooker and working areas in the kitchen cleaned.

There was still much to be done, but at least a start had been made, and the captain and the agent would be well aware that there was no way they would be allowed to leave the port until they had complied with Port Health's instructions.

'I've seen one or two like this,' Tom said as they trod carefully among the chaos. 'If we had any doubts about the importance of our job, these are the occasions that show how vital it is.'

'I agree,' she said soberly. 'When I was shown around your brother-in-law's ship the comparison between the two was so distressing, but when I tried

to explain that to him he brushed it aside, saying that
it was their own fault.'

Tom gave his dry laugh. 'What? *They* were to blame
for ignorance and poverty? He would! Peter hasn't
much time for bunglers and ineffectuals, and Herta
was the same. It may not be everyone's attitude, but it
certainly brought *them* prosperity.'

'He told me that I'm like her,' she said quietly, and
as he gazed at her in cold surprise she added quickly,
'In looks, that is.'

'Yes, you are like her in appearance,' he said slowly,
'but it ends there.'

'Meaning that I'm not a strong, efficient woman of
the world?'

Was there a glint of laughter in his eyes? She didn't
think so, not when they were on the subject of his
wife.

'You're a woman of the world all right, but shall we
say that *your* world moves on a different axis than hers
did? You are a normal, unselfish and uncomplicated
person. She was none of those things.'

'Her brother said something along those lines, which
surprised me,' she said cautiously, the unexpected
praise throwing her off balance.

'Yes,' he said heavily. 'Peter is nothing if not honest.
He calls a spade a spade. We get on well, although I
only see him rarely. I knew that the moment he
discovered that I'd transferred to the Port of
Manchester he would come knocking on my door and,
of course, he did.'

'And you weren't there.'

'Correct. I was in hospital, but we're not going to be
harking back to *that* misunderstanding, are we?'

'No. We'll hark back to one of the others for a change, shall we?' she said flippantly, and he sighed, bringing to mind the time when he had likened her behaviour to that of someone Lucy's age.

'Any more news from your mother?' he asked as they made their way back to Port House.

'No, not since yesterday. I imagine the next thing I hear will be the date and time for the wedding.'

'And where are you to be accommodated?' he said grimly. 'Your welfare is just as important as her wedding. You will be going all that way on your own. I hope she's considered that.'

Chloe laughed up at him. 'I doubt my mother would see any of it that way, but I *had* thought of taking a tent with me, just in case.'

'You're crazy,' he said, reaching out to move a strand of hair that the wind had blown across her face.

'It's the juvenile in me,' she said with teasing mockery. 'It makes me say and do unpredictable things, like this.' And in a moment of madness she reached up and kissed him hard on the mouth.

She was stepping back before he could take advantage of it, telling him, 'That was for the nice things you just said about me, and for being worried about where I will lay my head in New York.'

It had all been done with a sort of breezy cheek, and that was what she wanted him to see it as. If he guessed how moved she had been by the way he had described her, and by his concern for her safety when she went to the wedding, he might retreat from her again, and it could be once too many.

CHAPTER TEN

LORRAINE rang again over the weekend to inform Chloe that the wedding in two weeks' time would be at midday, in one of Manhattan's most fashionable churches.

She had to smile. That sounded about right for her mother. There was no way she could see her getting married in a tin mission hut.

'Don't wear cream,' Lorraine said, 'as I will be wearing it, and Edgar's three daughters have chosen pink, pale blue and that lovely shade of peppermint.'

'So I'm left with black, brown or purple,' Chloe joked, but her mother was not amused.

'It's a wedding. . .not a funeral!' she hissed angrily. 'You will be my only relative, so make sure you choose something appropriate.'

'Don't worry, I will,' Chloe assured her. 'The English contingent won't let you down.' That being so, Lorraine wasn't allowing her much time to shop for new clothes, just two weeks to prepare for a trip to America. There wouldn't be just an outfit for the wedding to choose, but leisure clothes and evening wear too.

Her mother hadn't mentioned how long she was expecting her to stay, and Chloe wasn't too bothered either way, except for the fact that as she had been with Port Health for only a short time there wouldn't be an awful lot of leave due to her. But this *was* a special occasion, and as such she wanted to give it its due.

Time to worry about what was going to happen at this end when she came back, but Chloe had already done one thing—a firm of estate agents were coming out one evening to value the apartment, and if the figure suggested met with Lorraine's approval, it would go on sale immediately, as the housing market was slow. Chloe felt that if there was going to be an upheaval in her life, the sooner it was accomplished, the better.

As if he had read her thoughts, Tom said on Monday morning, 'Do you want time off to go shopping for the wedding?'

She hesitated, not wanting any favours from him, but he *was* offering, and there was so little time. 'I wouldn't mind an afternoon, if that's all right with you?' she said.

'Yes, of course,' he agreed. 'I haven't any outside commitments this week, so I'll be on hand for any problems that arise.'

'Tomorrow, then?' she suggested.

'Yes, fine.'

Lucy came into the office later in the afternoon and Chloe realised that as the spring bank holiday was looming up she was off school.

'Dad tells me that you're going to a wedding in New York,' she said enviously. 'I wish it were me.'

'So do I,' Chloe told her glumly. 'I'm not bursting to be the odd one out in a gathering of wealthy Americans.'

'What are you going to wear?' Tom's daughter wanted to know.

'I've no idea at the moment,' Chloe told her. 'But hopefully by this time tomorrow the problem will have been solved. I've got the afternoon off to go shopping.'

'Can I come?' Lucy wheedled. 'I've got nothing to do, and I could tell you what suits you.'

Chloe laughed. 'I can manage that myself, but, yes, you can come if you want. When we've finished I'll take you for something to eat. We could even go to the cinema afterwards, if you like?'

'Of course I like!' Lucy whooped.

'All right, then,' Chloe told her. 'But you'd better make sure it's all right with your dad. If he agrees, you can stay the night. I'll use my mother's car in the morning to get us back to Eastham.'

'Yes, but how will we get to Manchester?' Lucy wanted to know. 'I'm too young to go on the back of the bike.'

'Yes, I *do* know that,' Chloe told her. 'Even if you weren't, I've a feeling that your father wouldn't approve.'

Tom came in at that moment, having been to say goodbye to his brother-in-law, whose ship was sailing on the afternoon tide. Chloe thought that she and Peter Hagenbaach hadn't got together again, after all. If he had been round to Tom's house to dine, she hadn't been invited. Considering Tom's reaction when he'd found them together, it wasn't surprising, and yet why? Why should it bother him if she sought the company of other men when he didn't want her himself?

Lucy immediately buttonholed him and proceeded to repeat Chloe's offer, the words tumbling out so fast that she was almost gabbling.

'Hold on a minute, Lucy,' he said. 'Say it again. . . and slowly.'

He was playing for time, Chloe thought, giving himself space before he had to come up with an answer. The misgivings she had felt the moment she had made the impulsive offer increased, because she wasn't sure if she was doing the right thing. If, for instance, Tom *did* marry Chantal Mortimer eventually, her own presence in their lives would be even more superfluous than it was now. To deepen the affection that was growing between Lucy and herself could hurt Saracen's daughter in the end, and Chloe would hate to do that.

However, he had his answer ready now, and it wasn't what she was expecting.

'How would it be if *I* drive you both into Manchester tomorrow afternoon, as I want to have another look at the coal handling set-up that I was telling you about at that end of the Ship Canal? If we both take our phones we can keep in touch, and once I've finished I'll join you in whichever store you're in. I need a suit, and I suppose it's as good a time as any to get it. Then *I'll* stand you both a meal, and *I'll* take you to the cinema.' Chloe stared at him in amazement as he concluded blandly, 'It's the least I can do after the way you helped us out while I was in hospital.'

As they strolled round the shops the following day Chloe asked Lucy casually, 'How are you getting on with Chantal at the moment?'

'No problem,' Lucy said airily. 'And do you know why?'

'No, I don't, but I bet you're going to tell me,' she teased.

'She's gone on holiday for a month, and is due back next weekend.'

'Ah, I see,' Chloe said slowly. So that explained why she hadn't been around when Tom was in hospital, and why he hadn't asked Chantal to be there for Lucy. He had said it was because his daughter wasn't keen on their attractive neighbour, but in light of what Lucy had just said it would seem more likely that it was because she wasn't available.

'And so who is in charge of the stables and riding school?' she asked.

'Her assistant, but Dad is keeping an eye on things, too.'

'Yes, I thought he might be,' she murmured. Deciding that she might allow herself just one more question, she asked, 'Did you see much of your uncle while he was here?'

'Yes,' Lucy said with a smile. 'He came to eat with us twice, and each time he was expecting *you* to be there. When he complained, Dad got edgy, and told Uncle Peter that he was old enough to be your father.'

'And what did he say to that?' Chloe asked curiously as a vision of the Dutchman's fair bearded face came to mind, with Tom's dark visage scowling in the background.

'He just laughed, and said so was Dad, and that he had never been able to see what was under his nose. I don't know what he meant by that, but Dad got really peeved then and told him that it was *his* family's fault that he'd got blinkered vision.'

'So they quarrelled?'

Lucy smiled. 'No, not really. They're too good friends for that, but Dad didn't say much afterwards.'

She would have liked to be a fly on the wall on that occasion, Chloe thought as they went into her mother's favourite store, and she didn't know whether to feel flattered or insulted that she'd been discussed like a prize in a lottery.

Her mobile phone rang as they were on the escalator and Tom's voice said, 'I've finished here. Where can I find you?'

She named a well-known store. 'In Ladies' Wear, needless to say.'

'Right. I'll find you there,' and he was gone.

After various forays in and out of the cubicles, steering clear of the colours that her mother had mentioned, Chloe decided to try on a caramel-coloured dress that was long and close-fitting with a high neck and long sleeves, and had a matching jerkin with just three buttons at breast height.

The moment she put it on she knew it was exactly right for her New York début. It was elegant, expensive. . .the first thing her mother would do would be to inspect the label. . .and the beautiful cool tone of the fabric blended perfectly with her colouring.

'So, what do I look like?' she asked of Lucy when she emerged from the cubicle.

'A stick of fudge,' she said with a grin.

'Fudge is soon gone,' Tom's voice said from a few feet away. 'How about butterscotch? It lasts forever.' His voice was soft, caressing almost, and Chloe became still.

'I'd decided that the colour was caramel,' she said after a moment's silence.

'Not caramel!' Lucy protested. 'It reminds me of Mrs Mortimer!'

Tom was frowning.

'Why does it remind you of Chantal?'

'Because it sticks when you don't want it to.'

His face tightened. Lucy had gone too far, and he said, 'You've maybe noticed that my daughter is inclined to be cheeky on occasion.'

Chloe, changing the subject, commented with a warning glance in Lucy's direction, 'Anyone would think we were discussing a sweet shop—fudge, butter-scotch and caramel.'

She felt happy and light-hearted for once with the three of them together, and she didn't want Lucy to spoil it, as the more she made clear her dislike of their neighbour, the more her father was likely to defend her. However miserable the thought of his friendship with Chantal made her, Chloe had to admit that on short acquaintance she had liked the woman.

'Whatever you decide to call it, you look very lovely,' Tom told her, his face clearing.

'Yes, well, they do say that clothes make the woman,' she said lightly. 'And you've only ever seen me in my biking gear or uniform.'

'And a black dress,' he reminded her. 'We mustn't forget that.'

No, indeed, she thought, her body warming in the knowledge that he hadn't forgotten that night on his launch, when the fog had been all around them, and he'd held her close for a few spellbinding seconds.

His eyes were holding hers, but they weren't giving anything away, and she wished crazily that a print-out of his thoughts would appear in them, but she had long

since accepted that there was no way she would ever
be able to read Tom Saracen's mind. Sufficient for
today was the fact that they had reached a new degree
of harmony.

He had a large carrier-bag with him, and she said in
amazement, 'You've already bought a suit!'

'Yes. I knew exactly what I wanted. The store had
it in stock in my size, it fitted perfectly. . .and here I
am. Once you've made *your* choice, we'll eat.'

Chloe had already made her choice the moment she
saw herself in the mirror, and if she'd had any doubts,
the fact that this man of few words thought she looked
lovely in it would have clinched the sale, even if it had
been two dishcloths sewn together.

To her surprise, Lucy didn't want to eat in one of
the fast-food places. They allowed her to choose, and
she guided them towards a smart Italian restaurant.

As they seated themselves Tom said in a low voice,
'Are you disappointed that you're not having a
hamburger?'

'Devastated,' Chloe laughed.

Lucy, studying the menu, looked over the top of it
to say pityingly, 'You adults always think that we
adolescents have no taste.'

They didn't go to the cinema. There was a fair in
Piccadilly Gardens, and the moment she saw it Lucy
was in favour of a change of plan. As they whizzed
around on the various rides, with raucous fairground
music churning out all around them, darkness was
falling and lights coming on all over the city.

Tom, sitting facing them in one of the hurtling
carriages, said, 'We must do this more often.'

His face had been in shadow as he spoke and Chloe couldn't tell which of them he was addressing, but she hoped it had included herself.

'Lucy can come home with me,' he said when they eventually left the fair in the floodlit gardens. 'There is no need for her to inconvenience you while I'm here with the car.'

That didn't go down too well with Lucy, so Chloe suggested, 'Why don't we all go back to the apartment for coffee and decide what we're going to do then?'

'Yes, that would be nice,' he said. 'I'd like to see where you live.'

When they got out of the car and stood on the forecourt of the apartment block, Tom gave an impressed whistle.

'Very palatial,' he said. 'It didn't really register with me the night I dropped you off after the pop concert, but tonight we see it in all its glory!'

'Beauty is in the eye of the beholder, don't forget,' she reminded him with a smile. 'Wait until you see all my mother's décor!'

Lucy had walked away from them to the pavement, intrigued by the sound of disco music coming from near by, and as she looked at the figure of the young girl, and eyed the tall man at her side, Chloe was thinking what a lovely day it had been. Except for those few seconds when Lucy had been rude about Chantal, they had all been relaxed and happy, and she didn't want it to end.

She started to move towards Lucy, to coax her away from the sounds of the city. Just as she drew level with her Chloe saw that the driver of a car that was only feet away from them had slumped over the wheel, and the vehicle was swerving towards them, mounting the pavement as it did so. Then it was on top of them, and there was no time to back away. The bonnet was only inches from them, and with an almighty frantic heave she pushed Lucy to safety, only to find there was no time to save herself.

As it pinned her up against the wall of the building next to the apartment all she could hear were Lucy's screams and Tom's voice bellowing near by, and then the pain came, hot searing agony in her legs and all down the front of her.

When Chloe opened her eyes, it wasn't hard to guess where she was, even though the room seemed to be full of mist—there were bottles and drips, an oxygen cylinder, and a medicine trolley at one side of the bed. At the other side was Lucy, head bent, crying into a handkerchief.

'Don't,' Chloe said weakly. 'Don't!'

Lucy's head came up at that, and the tears stopped, and somewhere near by Chloe heard an official-sounding voice saying sombrely, 'We think we will be able to save the leg, but your fiancée will have lasting scar tissue, I'm afraid.'

Lucy had gone, and Chloe could hear whispering and rustling noises near by. She wondered fuzzily who they were talking about. It couldn't be herself as *she* wasn't anybody's fiancée. Then Lucy was back again with a smile on her swollen lips, and, delight of delights, Tom was with her, looking gaunt and unshaven.

A doctor and nurse were at the other side of the bed, observing her with professional gravity, but Tom wasn't taking any notice of them. His eyes were riveted on her face and he was saying hoarsely, 'Chloe! Thank God you've come back to me!'

She frowned. 'Why? Where have I been?'

'In some distant place where I couldn't reach you,' he said raggedly.

'You're mistaken,' she chided drowsily. 'I haven't been to America yet.'

'No, you haven't, but you've been unconscious for two days.'

The mists were clearing now, and with their going she realised that she was hurting, badly, especially in one of her legs. She began to moan softly, and the doctor said quickly, 'If you and your daughter would like to wait outside for a few moments, Mr Saracen, we are going to give Chloe some medication.'

A long time later she woke again. Her mother was asleep in a chair by the bed, and Chloe decided that she must be dying if Lorraine had come back home, but the nurse who came bustling in at that moment didn't seem too concerned about her as she said brightly, 'Ah, you're awake, Chloe. Feel better after that good sleep?'

Suddenly she felt weepy, and knew it was because Tom wasn't there, and as she drifted off again she wondered if he was keeping his eye on the Nigerian ship.

After that some of the days were hazy, some clear, but whatever sort of a day it was she was aware that during some part of it Tom was by her side. Usually it was in the evening, as he still had to take care of Port Health during the day, and sometimes he brought Lucy with him.

Each time she saw him coming through the door she didn't feel so weak, and the pain wasn't quite so bad. There was always raw anxiety in his eyes, and she tried to reassure him, to make him see that this dreadful time would come to an end, but her natural fluency seemed to have deserted her, and all she could whisper was, 'It's all right. Don't worry. I'll soon be well.' He would shake his head as if a message from the Almighty Himself wouldn't be enough to convince him of that.

'You saved Lucy,' he'd said to her on more than one occasion, his voice breaking.

She had squeezed his hand and murmured smilingly, 'Yes. Aren't I a clever girl?' before drifting off to sleep again.

Her mother came in the afternoons, and hadn't once mentioned having to cancel her wedding, which gave Chloe some idea of how badly she'd been hurt, and if she'd had any doubts a chat with the consultant on one of her better days would have confirmed it.

'Your left leg was almost severed by the front bumper of the car,' he told her. 'We had to sort out arteries, blood vessels, and stitch damaged tissue together. Your ribs are broken, and you have a fractured elbow and collarbone, along with sundry deep gashes across the abdomen, but the thing that is making you feel so ill at the moment is shock, delayed shock.'

He smiled.

'And, having said all that, it could have been a lot worse. I'm afraid that you're going to be with us for some weeks, and it will be months before your leg is anywhere near back to normal, but you're getting there. You're going to be all right.'

He continued, 'I thought that we were going to have

three patients on our hands the night you were brought in. The young girl was hysterical, and your fiancé so traumatised with horror that I thought he would have collapsed, but, of course, he didn't. Men of that calibre can usually cope, and he did.'

When he had gone Chloe lay gazing up at the ward ceiling and went over everything he'd said in her mind. His description of her injuries was no surprise, the degree of pain and weakness were proof of that, but the consultant had surprised her on one point: he referred to Tom as her fiancé, and her thoughts went back to those first few minutes after she had regained consciousness. They had been discussing somebody's fiancée then, but there had been no reason why she should have thought they were talking about her.

A tear slid down her cheek. Tom must have told the hospital staff that she and he were engaged, so they would let him stay, as he could hardly have claimed to be next of kin. That had to be the reason, and how she wished it wasn't. He had never mentioned it, and she wasn't going to either, not until she could discuss it with him coherently.

Eventually there came a warm Saturday afternoon, when she'd had her physiotherapy session, managed to eat a reasonable lunch, had a shower and washed her hair, and was waiting for him on a bench in the hospital gardens beside the ward.

The stick that she used was beside her. Tom had turned up with it when she had become mobile again— a rod of fine polished wood with a wide bone handle fashioned in the shape of the old mythical sea dog Cerebos, as outlined on his Port Health tie.

Her face flushed with pleasure at the memory of the

moment when he had given it to her. She had been delighted to receive it, acclaiming the thought that had gone into the gift, and for a brief moment the anxiety had left his eyes.

And now, today, she was ready to talk to him properly for the first time in weeks. She was going to urge him to forget what had happened that night, to move forward instead of back, in whatever direction he wanted to take. The poor man in the car that had struck her had suffered a fatal heart attack, and for someone that was a sorrow much greater than his or hers.

He needed to know that the anguish that never left him, because she had almost got herself killed saving Lucy, had to be put to one side, banished, because she would do it all over again if she had to.

And it hadn't all been doom and gloom, either. For one thing she had discovered that beneath her restless exterior her mother *did* care about her. That, although she found it hard to show affection, it was there. Perhaps to a lesser degree than Grace Saracen's for her son, but there nevertheless. It was just very sad that she'd had to be almost at death's door to be shown it, just as she'd had to be in that state for Tom to declare her to be his fiancée.

Well, today she was going to tell him she knew what he'd done. . .and why. She was going to let him off the hook before he started wriggling, and when her mother came later she was going to insist that she return to New York without delay to carry on with her deferred wedding arrangements.

Tom was coming, making his way purposefully along the path between the lawns and flowerbeds, brow furrowed, mouth unsmiling, and thinner than before her accident.

When he looked up and saw her waiting in a pale blue silk dressing-gown over matching pyjamas his face cleared and his step quickened.

'Chloe!' he said buoyantly. 'What a lovely surprise! How long have you been waiting?'

There was sadness in her smile. All my life, she wanted to say, but there had to be no complications today, just a straightforward discussion, and so she said, 'Only a matter of minutes. I guessed you might be arriving about now.'

He had brought flowers and chocolates, and after he'd laid them on the seat beside her he stood looking down on to her pale face. 'Are you sure you should be out here?' he asked.

She laughed. 'Yes, of course. I'm almost better now. Another week and I'm to be discharged.'

His face lit up. 'Really?'

'Yes, really, and before I go home there is something I have to say to you. Something I should have said before, but I just couldn't get my mind together.'

'What is it?' he asked, his face sobering.

She took a deep breath. 'I know that you've told the people here that we're engaged, so that you wouldn't be stopped from visiting me, and I also know why you've been so desperate to be with me.'

'You do?'

'Yes. It's because you feel so guilty at my getting hurt because of Lucy.'

He opened his mouth to speak, but she put out her hand to stop him.

'Let me finish, please. I want you to know that there

is no cause for you to feel so guilty. I've been trying to make you understand that all along. The way the accident occurred wasn't your fault, Lucy's, or that of the poor man whose heart stopped beating. The fates decreed that we should all be where we were at that particular moment.'

'They didn't decree that you should risk your life for Lucy!' he argued grimly.

'No, maybe not, but was I supposed to stand by and watch a helpless child killed? *You* wouldn't have, would you? And neither could I. So will you please stop feeling you have to atone for what I did? You once told me in no uncertain terms that you didn't want sympathy, or charity, and in this instance. . . neither do I.'

There *was* something she wanted. . .desperately, but she didn't think he had it to give, and in the meantime she was going to have to forget it and concentrate on clearing the air between them.

'Have you quite finished?' he was asking,

'Er—yes.'

'And *I* can say something now?'

'Yes,' she said slowly.

'Right. First of all, with regard to my passing myself off as your fiancé, it wasn't done out of the kindness of my heart.'

'No?'

'No. I said that because it was what I wanted to be the truth, and I've got something in my jacket pocket to prove it. Like a stupid fool I hadn't been able to admit it until I nearly lost you. So, you see, it wasn't because I thought they wouldn't let me stay with you that I said it. During those first few days there wasn't a power on earth that would have shifted me.

'I *do* feel guilty and anguished that you sacrificed yourself for Lucy, but again, that's not the reason why I'm never away from this place. It's because I love you, Chloe, deeply and desperately, and I think. . .I pray. . .that you love me.

'It's been hellish trying not to give in to my longing for you, being with you in the office or on the docks, day after day, but how could I ask someone as young and unspoilt as yourself to become saddled with a widower with a teenage daughter?

'In the end it was no use. I *have* to ask you. I've been waiting until you were strong enough, and maybe now you are. Will you marry me?'

She was laughing now, joyous peals that made heads turn among other patients and visitors enjoying the sunshine, and he said unsteadily, 'What is it?'

'You're asking me if I'd be willing to take on you and Lucy, but what about the bargain *you'd* be getting. . .a mass of broken bones and a gammy leg?'

'It wouldn't be a bargain,' he said softly. 'It would be a gift. . .a gift from the gods.'

'Is that really how you feel?' she asked wonderingly.

'Yes, it is. It's the way I've felt from the moment I met you, and I've never stopped wanting you since, in my arms, my bed, and in my heart, forever.'

He put one arm gently around her thin shoulders, and tilted her face up to his with the other.

'So what do you say, Chloe?'

'I say yes,' she whispered laughingly. 'If only to escape becoming a nun.'

He eyed her with amusement, and lifted a strand of her hair with a tender finger.

'It would be a crime to cover this up, but I thought your future plans were based on a cottage at Pickering's Lock, and a rowing boat therewith. Which brings me to the question—will you be able to settle for my house at Eastham?'

'But of course,' she assured him gaily. 'Pickering's Lock was my second choice. Your place was the first, but it was a case of waiting for an invitation, and there didn't seem much chance of that. I thought that Chantal had got in first, and that made me miserable enough, but what was worse, when I met the woman I really liked her, and felt she was just your type.'

Tom shook his head. 'No, she wasn't. My type was a clever young miss who'd got herself a job with Port Health, and was going to be very good at it. She was forever on my mind, and because of that I tried to keep her at arm's length, when all the time I wanted her *in* my arms.'

Thomas sighed, but the happiness in his face belied it. 'There was every chance in the world of your being invited into my home on a permanent basis, but I kept pretending there wasn't. Even though on the day of the accident I'd bought a morning suit.'

She looked at him with surprised melting eyes.

'So you were *that* sure of me, even if you had doubts about yourself?'

He laughed, and told her tenderly, 'I wasn't so conceited that I'd have bought a suit for my wedding before I'd even proposed. It was for America. . .for your mother's wedding.'

'America?' she repeated.

'Yes. I was determined that, invited or not, I was going with you. I couldn't bear the thought of your being isolated out there, with nobody caring a damn, but, having seen quite a lot of your mother in recent weeks I've found her softer than I expected.'

'So have I,' she said radiantly, and looking down at her leg. 'Which means that lots of wonderful things have come out of the accident.'

'Yes,' he agreed sombrely. 'It took a horrendous thing like that to bring me to my senses. When I thought I was going to lose you I nearly went out of my mind at the thought of the way I'd been pussyfooting about all these weeks, playing hard to get, when I wanted you so desperately.'

His voice roughened, and with a sudden desperate urgency he said, 'And, talking about the senses. . .kiss me, Chloe. Do you remember my saying that once before? It was for a different reason then. I was calling what I thought was your bluff. Today, I'm asking you to kiss me because you're so frail, and I'm afraid of hurting you.'

'Nothing can hurt me now,' she told him triumphantly, and as she reached up and brought his head down to hers and kissed him long and passionately it was as if the heartache and yearning had never been. His strength seemed to be flowing into her, his desire was matching the flame inside her, and his tenderness was the most wonderful thing she had ever known.

When they drew apart he said softly, 'You remember I said that I had proof of my honourable intentions? Something I've been carrying around for weeks?'

'Yes, I remember,' she said contentedly. 'What is it?'

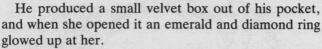

He produced a small velvet box out of his pocket, and when she opened it an emerald and diamond ring glowed up at her.

'Put it on,' he commanded gently, 'so that I can look the hospital staff in the eye.'

It was a month later, and a flight for New York had just been called in the terminal at Manchester Airport. At the announcement a tall dark man and fair-haired woman leaning on a stick left their seats and began to make their way to where the plane was waiting. They had eyes only for each other, and to the curious onlooker it would seem that, although they weren't touching, they were as one.

They would be in America for just a few days as guests at a fashionable wedding, and then would return to where a teenage girl, who had been staying with friends, eagerly awaited them.

In a short time there would be another wedding, with the bride and groom from New York among those present. This time it would be a wedding with a difference.

After the ceremony the newlyweds, along with their dark-haired bridesmaid, would sail along the Ship Canal in the bridegroom's launch to join the rest of the party for a reception on a gaily painted pleasure boat on the River Weaver, an arrangement that was only fitting for two people whose working life, on and about those same waters, had brought them love and happiness.

4 new short romances all wrapped up in 1 sparkling volume.

Join four delightful couples as they journey home for the festive season—and discover the true meaning of Christmas...that love is the best gift of all!

A Man To Live For - Emma Richmond

Yule Tide - Catherine George

Mistletoe Kisses - Lynsey Stevens

Christmas Charade - Kay Gregory

Available: November 1995   **Price: £4.99**

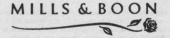

MILLS & BOON

GET 4 BOOKS AND A MYSTERY GIFT

Return this coupon and we'll send you 4 Love on Call novels and a mystery gift absolutely FREE! We'll even pay the postage and packing for you.

We're making you this offer to introduce you to the benefits of Reader Service: FREE home delivery of brand-new Love on Call novels, at least a month before they are available in the shops, FREE gifts and a monthly Newsletter packed with information.

Accepting these FREE books and gift places you under no obligation to buy, you may cancel at any time, even after receiving just your free shipment. Simply complete the coupon below and send it to:

MILLS & BOON READER SERVICE, FREEPOST, CROYDON, SURREY, CR9 3WZ.

No stamp needed

Yes, please send me 4 free Love on Call novels and a mystery gift. I understand that unless you hear from me, I will receive 4 superb new titles every month for just £1.99* each postage and packing free. I am under no obligation to purchase any books and I may cancel or suspend my subscription at any time, but the free books and gifts will be mine to keep in any case. (I am over 18 years of age)

2EP5D

Ms/Mrs/Miss/Mr _____

Address _____

_____

_____ Postcode _____